Slayed by Darkness

Also From Alexandra Ivy

GUARDIANS OF ETERNITY
WHEN DARKNESS ENDS
EMBRACE THE DARKNESS
DARKNESS EVERLASTING
DARKNESS REVEALED
DARKNESS UNLEASHED
BEYOND THE DARKNESS
DEVOURED BY DARKNESS
BOUND BY DARKNESS
FEAR THE DARKNESS
DARKNESS AVENGED
HUNT THE DARKNESS
WHEN DARKNESS COMES
DARKNESS RETURNS
BEWARE THE DARKNESS
CONQUER THE DARKNESS
SACRAFICE OF DARKNESS
SHADES OF DARKNESS
DARKNESS BETRAYED

BAYOU HEAT SERIES
RAPHAEL/PARISH
BAYON/JEAN-BAPTISTE
TALON/XAVIER
SEBASTIAN/ARISTIDE
LIAN/ROCH
HAKAN/SEVERIN
ANGEL/HISS
RAGE/KILLIAN (1001 DARK NIGHTS)
MICHEL/STRIKER
ICE/REAUX
KAYDEN/SIMON (1001 DARK NIGHTS)
BLADE (1001 DARK NIGHTS)

THE IMMORTAL ROGUES
MY LORD VAMPIRE

MY LORD ETERNITY
MY LORD IMMORTALITY

THE SENTINELS
BORN IN BLOOD
BLOOD ASSASSIN
BLOOD LUST

ARES SECURITY
KILL WITHOUT MERCY
KILL WITHOUT SHAME

HISTORICAL ROMANCE
SOME LIKE IT WICKED
SOME LIKE IT SINFUL
SOME LIKE IT BRAZEN

ROMANTIC SUSPENSE
PRETEND YOU'RE SAFE
WHAT ARE YOU AFRAID OF?
YOU WILL SUFFER
THE INTENDED VICTIM
DON'T LOOK

Slayed by Darkness

A Guardians of Eternity Novella

By Alexandra Ivy

1001 DARK NIGHTS
PRESS

Slayed by Darkness
A Guardians of Eternity Novella
By Alexandra Ivy

1001 Dark Nights

Copyright 2021 Debbie Raleigh
ISBN: 978-1-951812-37-9

Foreword: Copyright 2014 M. J. Rose

Published by 1001 Dark Nights Press, an imprint of Evil Eye Concepts, Incorporated

Sign up for the 1001 Dark Nights Newsletter
and be entered to win a Tiffany Key necklace.

There's a contest every month!

Go to www.1001DarkNights.com to subscribe.

**As a bonus, all subscribers can download
FIVE FREE exclusive books!**

Acknowledgments from the Author

To all my fabulous readers! Better times ahead.

One Thousand and One Dark Nights

Once upon a time, in the future…

*I was a student fascinated with stories and learning.
I studied philosophy, poetry, history, the occult, and
the art and science of love and magic. I had a vast
library at my father's home and collected thousands
of volumes of fantastic tales.*

*I learned all about ancient races and bygone
times. About myths and legends and dreams of all
people through the millennium. And the more I read
the stronger my imagination grew until I discovered
that I was able to travel into the stories... to actually
become part of them.*

*I wish I could say that I listened to my teacher
and respected my gift, as I ought to have. If I had, I
would not be telling you this tale now.
But I was foolhardy and confused, showing off
with bravery.*

*One afternoon, curious about the myth of the
Arabian Nights, I traveled back to ancient Persia to
see for myself if it was true that every day Shahryar
(Persian: شهريار, "king") married a new virgin, and then
sent yesterday's wife to be beheaded. It was written
and I had read that by the time he met Scheherazade,
the vizier's daughter, he'd killed one thousand
women.*

*Something went wrong with my efforts. I arrived
in the midst of the story and somehow exchanged
places with Scheherazade — a phenomena that had
never occurred before and that still to this day, I
cannot explain.*

*Now I am trapped in that ancient past. I have
taken on Scheherazade's life and the only way I can
protect myself and stay alive is to do what she did to
protect herself and stay alive.*

*Every night the King calls for me and listens as I spin tales.
And when the evening ends and dawn breaks, I stop at a
point that leaves him breathless and yearning for more.
And so the King spares my life for one more day, so that
he might hear the rest of my dark tale.*

*As soon as I finish a story... I begin a new
one... like the one that you, dear reader, have before
you now.*

Prologue

Moscow
1237 AD

It was more luck than planning that brought Jayla to Moscow during the invasion of the Mongolian Golden Horde. The chaos of the ruthless siege meant she could move through the battered city unnoticed.

There was nothing like plundering, pillaging, and massive carnage to provide a distraction.

Blending with the shadows, Jayla avoided the wooden houses and thatched roofs being torched by the invaders. Not only because vampires and fire didn't mix, but she couldn't risk being seen by hidden watchers.

The ultimate rule of an assassin was to be invisible. And that's what she was.

Silent death.

Jayla slowed as she caught an unmistakable chill beneath her feet. The thick layer of ice and snow that coated the cobblestone street wasn't the cause. It was a subtle warning that crawled beneath the ground and spread throughout the neighborhood. Any demon in the area would know a vampire's lair was nearby. And if they had a brain, they would turn around and scurry away.

Following the chill toward a house on the edge of the city, she eyed the structure with a lift of her brows. It looked more like a fortress than a home with thick stone walls, narrow, heavily shuttered windows, and a steeply angled roof currently coated in snow. A human had no doubt built it to protect those inside from the cold, as well as from any invaders, but it was a perfect lair for a vampire. No sunlight, no chance of fire, and few access points.

Jayla did a quick circle around the building, searching for any hidden traps. The second rule of being an assassin was: Don't get caught.

Once satisfied, Jayla chose a narrow door at the back to enter. She waited for a pair of human soldiers to scurry past before wading through the snow to the door. If they had glanced in her direction, they wouldn't have noticed more than a small figure wrapped in a heavy woolen robe with the hood pulled over her head. Just another beggar. But the third rule of being an assassin: Leave no witnesses.

Once they were gone, Jayla tossed off the robe. Now that she was at her destination, she didn't need a disguise. She needed speed. The thick material of the robe hampered her movements.

Pushing open the door, she stepped into the cramped vestibule. It was a small, dark space with a low, open-beamed roof and stone floor. There was a fireplace, but it was empty, leaving a frigid bite in the air. Jayla didn't mind. It would take her hours to wash the stench of the burning city from her skin.

Scanning the darkness, Jayla wasn't surprised to discover a vampire standing guard in front of the opening leading deeper into the house. Azrael was rumored to be the most lethal mercenary among all vampires. He wouldn't make it easy for her to sneak up on him.

Thankfully, her arrival caught the male by surprise. And, as usual, the sight of her lulled her opponent into a false sense of complacency. When they looked at her, they saw a female who was as small and delicate as a dew fairy. Her raven-black hair was twisted into elaborate knots and held in place with jade ornaments. Her dark green eyes and the lush temptation of her ruby lips dominated her golden, oval face. A short silk tunic that revealed her slender legs and a jade pendant hanging around her slender throat completed her fragile appearance.

The male blinked, peering through his shaggy brown hair that hadn't been combed in the past few decades. Probably the same time he'd last bothered to take a bath. Whatever his talents, they didn't include personal hygiene.

"Who are you?" he growled, prowling forward.

"A gift." She offered a disarming smile. "For Azrael."

The male narrowed his muddy brown eyes. "From who?"

Jayla hesitated. Should she lie? No. It was always better to stay as close to the truth as possible. Less opportunity to get tripped up later.

"The Anasso."

The male stiffened. The King of Vampires instilled equal parts respect and fear among his people. "Why would he send a gift?"

"The Anasso has been impressed by the rumors of such an impressive fighter. He sent me to express his admiration."

Warily, the guard inched forward. "How do I know you're not a Trojan horse?"

Jayla frowned. What was he...? Ah. She belatedly recalled the tactical ploy by the Greek humans to conquer the city of Troy.

Her lips twitched. The male might smell as if he'd climbed out of a dunghill, but he was smarter than he looked—a reminder not to underestimate her opponent.

She spread her arms, her lips pursed into a pout. "Do I look like a horse?"

Lust smoldered in the guard's eyes as he halted in front of her, but he remained suspicious. "Strip," he commanded.

She blinked as if confused. "Excuse me?"

"I need to make sure you're not hiding any weapons."

"Fine." Slowly turning, she glanced over her shoulder. "You'll have to undo the fastenings."

The guard released a growl of anticipation, his gaze locked on the tiny buttons that ran down the length of her dress. He seemed to forget all about his duties as a guard as he prowled forward, his fangs fully extended.

Lifting her arms as if preparing to allow the silky garment to be pulled over her head, she discreetly pulled one of the ornaments from her hair, revealing the thin, silver blade. Oblivious to the danger, the guard reached out to grab the back of her dress, his foul scent making her gag. Impatient to be done with the fool, Jayla whirled, her arm moving in a smooth arc as she turned.

"Hey—" The male's protest was cut short as her hand impacted, and the blade slid directly into his heart.

There was a choked sound of shock as the vampire glanced down at the elegant weapon sticking out of his chest. Then, falling to his knees, he toppled forward like a tree that had rotted at the core.

Stepping over his body already crumbling to ash, Jayla headed through the entryway to the main room. She halted to glance around the open space with its lofted ceiling and flagstone floor. There was a massive fireplace across the room and a long dining table that could seat at least a dozen guests, along with iron racks that held spears, shields, and rusted swords—all unnecessary items for a vampire. They didn't need heat, they didn't eat their meals off a plate, and their weapons were never allowed to rust.

Was this a temporary lair?

She was still pondering the question when a thunderous energy sizzled through the air. Azrael. No other creature could possess that much power. Well, no one beyond the Anasso. Jayla grabbed a second ornament from her hair. This one had the same slender silver blade, along with a powerful curse.

Moments later, a tall male with silvery blond hair cut close to his head and piercing blue eyes entered the room. Jayla gasped. He was…stunning. Even for a vampire—who were always gorgeous.

His face was exquisite perfection. From the wide brow and high, angular cheekbones to the arrogant length of his narrow nose. His mouth was wide and curved into a sensuous smile. Her gaze slid downward, taking in the tattoo that wound around the side of his neck. Were those feathers? And then farther down to the broad, naked chest that narrowed to a slender waist. Her mouth went dry, half expecting him to be fully exposed. She felt a pang of disappointment to discover that he wore heavy leather leggings and boots laced up to his knees.

He reminded her of a lethal Siberian tiger, all sleek muscles and coiled power.

Elegant death preparing to pounce.

Stalking forward, he pulled a slender sword free of the sheath hooked around his waist. "I've been expecting you," he drawled. "Jayla, I presume?"

Sensations clawed through Jayla. Not fear that he'd known she was coming or that he knew her name—she was always prepared for any contingency. No, this was a different unease.

It was awareness. A deep, shockingly intense connection to this male that she'd never encountered before. As if destiny had just punched her in the gut.

Jayla hissed. How was it possible? Was it a trick?

Yes, that had to be it.

She held on to the lame explanation, spreading her feet as he strolled to stand directly in front of her.

"I don't know whether to be pleased or insulted that you expected me and yet chose to surround yourself with such incompetent guards," she taunted.

He shrugged, his muscles rippling beneath his pale, satin-smooth skin. "They are temporary guards who came with the house. Unlike your Anasso, I don't have the desire to enslave my fellow vampires to create an empire."

She twirled the blade in her hand. Was he trying to distract her? She could have told him the sight of his raw male beauty was already scrambling her brain.

"You think I'm enslaved?" With a blinding motion, Jayla darted forward, aiming the dagger at Azrael's heart.

The male easily avoided the blow, slashing his sword through the air to drive her backward.

"I assume you willingly joined the cause," he mocked. "But what do you suppose would happen if you chose to walk away?"

Jayla stepped to the side, telling herself the strange cramping in her stomach was because of his obvious skill as a warrior and not the niggling concern lodged in the back of her mind. Her doubts about the King of Vampires were a worry for another time and place.

"I'd walk away," she said with more confidence than she felt.

"You don't believe that. I can see it in your eyes."

His absolute certainty pissed her off. She feinted to the left before whirling to the side, trying to plunge her dagger into his back. Even if she missed his heart, the silver in the blade should slow him down.

"If you think you can convince me to join your rebellion…" Her words trailed away as she caught sight of the glorious tattoo spread across his shoulders and down his spine.

Angel wings.

She didn't have time for more than a glimpse before he spun, the sword nearly taking off her head as she fell to her knees.

"Rebellion." He didn't press his attack. Instead, he sent her a mocking smile. "Is that what he told you?"

She slashed the dagger at his legs, forcing him back so she could jump to her feet. "Why else would I be here?"

"Because he fears I might reveal the nasty bargain he offered me."

They walked in a slow circle, like two dancers moving to a song only they could hear.

Jayla frowned. "What bargain?"

"He demanded that I kill the clan chief of Thebes."

She made a sound of disgust. If he were going to lie, then he should have taken more care to choose one she might believe.

"Leonidas has bent the knee, swearing his allegiance to the king. Why would he want him destroyed?"

"Because he has amassed a fortune that your king not only wants in his treasury, but fears could be used against him if Leonidas decides to challenge him for the throne." He twirled the sword, his expression annoyingly confident. "And, more importantly, the Anasso lusts after Leonidas's mate."

"A lie." With a flick of her wrist, Jayla sent one of her daggers flying toward the taunting male. It wasn't only a way to knock him off guard. It was a chance to interrupt his accusations that were stirring suspicions she didn't want roused.

Azrael knocked aside the dagger with his sword. "Believe what you want. The Anasso arrived here several days ago with a treasure chest and a demand that I take care of his dirty business. When I said no, I assumed he would try and silence me. "

Jayla clutched the cursed dagger that she'd been careful to keep. She just had to get close enough to stick it in his heart.

"Why you?"

"Because I'm the best." He didn't sound arrogant. Just certain that he was truly the best.

Jayla narrowed her eyes, taking a step closer to the male. "You aren't a part of our clan. If the Anasso wanted a rival clan chief dead, he would come to me. I am his personal assassin."

"He didn't want you to know because he knew it would reveal that he isn't the glorious hero he pretends to be."

She scowled. There was an edge of calm sincerity to his voice that undermined her attempt to convince herself that he was crafting some elaborate lie. Grimly, she forced herself to take another step closer. She needed to end this. Now.

"You're a mercenary." She didn't have to pretend to be interested in his answer, her feet taking her relentlessly closer to him. Close enough to catch his scent. The rich musk of a wild, untamed creature. "Why didn't you accept his offer?"

He lifted one shoulder. "At this moment, I just want to live in peace."

"Peace?" Jayla cocked her head to the side, deliberately pausing to listen to the violent commotion outside. "Forgive me if I find that hard to believe."

"I have no control over the Golden Horde."

She spread her arms wide, the dagger mere inches from his chest. "You're just an innocent victim of circumstances, eh?"

The impossibly blue eyes shimmered with amusement. "I have never been innocent, and anyone who imagines I could be a victim usually ends up dead."

"Usually?" Another step closer.

"Always."

Clenching her muscles, she prepared to attack. It was now or never. "I love cutting an arrogant male down to size," she murmured.

"Stop." The voice echoed deep inside her, halting her mid-leap. This is not your fight, *kiska*. Return to your home."

She clenched her teeth, fighting against the compulsion that held her prisoner. Most vampires could control humans and some lesser demons by seizing their minds. But only a rare few could compel a vampire. It was no wonder Azrael was such a successful mercenary. And why he'd allowed her to enter his lair so easily.

"No," she hissed, her muscles trembling as she fought against the urgent need to obey his commands.

He frowned as if surprised by her stubborn resistance. "I don't want to hurt you. Leave and don't return."

"I…can't." Calling on the skills she'd learned during her years of training, Jayla shattered his powerful grasp on her mind, calling on her secret power. The energy she released didn't send the male reeling backwards or screaming in pain. Instead, Azrael stood in motionless silence, temporarily frozen in time.

Then, before she could consider the terrible consequences, she leaped forward, stabbing her cursed dagger into the center of his heart.

The blade slid deep as time lurched back into motion, and she jumped backward. Azrael's eyes widened as if he belatedly realized precisely what had happened. But it was too late. The sword dropped from his hand, and he fell to the floor. Jayla swallowed a cry of dismay, the image of his golden perfection seared into her brain, even as she watched the darkness crawl over his body, turning him to ash.

Jayla prodded herself to leave. There were other guards in the lair. She could sense them. And, eventually, they would come in search of their master. Instead, she dropped to her knees. She'd done exactly what she had come to do: destroy the male who'd threatened her king.

The last thing she expected to feel was as if she'd stabbed the dagger into her own heart.

Reaching up, Jayla grabbed the jade pendant hanging around her neck. With a quick yank, she broke the golden chain. Then, pressing a kiss to the delicate talisman her maker had given to her the day she became a vampire, she laid it next to the sword.

"Forgive me…"

Chapter 1

Hong Kong
Present Day

Jayla's penthouse office on the top of Dreamscape Resorts offered a number of perks. It was the size of most local apartments and furnished in brilliant shades of crimson and gold. Best of all, it had a glass wall that offered a stunning view of the city skyline and the nearby Victoria Harbour.

There had to be some payoff for the aggravation of managing a resort that catered to endless hordes of customers during the year and employed nearly a thousand workers—both human and demon. She loved the challenge, but she was in dire need of *me-time* each evening to soothe her nerves.

Now, she sat next to the glass wall, a small lacquer table set in front of her. On the table was a tray, precisely arranged with her pink and green floral tea set. She'd just finished pouring hot water over the bone china, warming it in the traditional manner, before reaching for the canister of tea. She raised it to her nose to savor the rich scent before scooping it into the perfectly heated teapot. Allowing it to steep, she cleared her mind. This wasn't time to dwell on problems or consider the future. It was an opportunity to savor her momentary peace. Once the tea was ready, Jayla poured the hot liquid into a snifter. Once again, she lifted it to appreciate the aroma before carefully pouring it into the teacup.

She'd just settled back in her soft leather chair to take a sip when the door to the office opened.

"Excuse me."

A chill blasted through the air as she reluctantly turned her head to discover her assistant, Gideon, stepping into the room. The tall, slender vampire's hair was a deep red and cut short, his eyes a bright hazel dusted with gold. His features were delicate but unmistakably male with a bold nose and square jaw. His smile, however, made him a favorite among the human guests. It was wide and welcoming without any hint of the torture he'd suffered in the slave pits of a brutal vampire who'd considered his clansmen to be nothing more than objects to be used and abused.

"Gideon." Jayla slid a pointed glance over his tailored black suit paired with a crisp white shirt and gray silk tie.

Gideon stopped in the center of the room, his expression wary. "Yes?"

"Do you find me a demanding employer?" Her voice was so soft, the male was forced to lean forward as he strained to hear her.

He swallowed as if he had a lump in his throat. "No, mistress."

"Do I have an excessive number of unreasonable rules?"

"No, mistress."

She held the vampire's gaze, her face carefully devoid of emotion. Unlike his previous master, she didn't lead by fear or intimidation. She simply shared her expectations. Either the employee lived up to those expectations, or they found a new job.

Until this moment, Gideon had rarely disappointed her. That was one of the reasons he'd become her most trusted assistant. That, and his absolute, unshakable loyalty.

"What is my one request?"

"That you are not interrupted during your teatime."

She arched a brow. "And yet, here you are."

He grimaced, knowing her too well to mistake her calm tone for anything but a sharp reprimand.

"I would never bother you if it wasn't urgent."

"Is the hotel on fire?"

"No."

"Is one of the customers dead?"

"No, but…"

"Go away." She waved her hand toward the door.

"It's Emile," he said in a rush. "From the Paradise."

Jayla carefully replaced her teacup on the tray and rose to her feet. Emile was her nemesis. It sounded melodramatic. Maybe childish. But there it was.

The female vampire had been the owner of an established resort when Chiron had decided to expand his business to Hong Kong. Not surprisingly, she'd done her best to keep Dreamscape from opening, including issuing a direct threat against Jayla. It'd been the local clan chief who halted any battles, announcing there was plenty of customers for both resorts to thrive. He'd also warned that any challenges or dirty tricks, and he would run the offender out of town.

"She's here?" Jayla demanded in disbelief, the walls frosting over as she struggled to contain her temper. The two vampires had gone to great lengths to avoid crossing paths. The thought that the bitch would enter Jayla's territory was infuriating.

"No. She sent an emissary."

That explained why Jayla hadn't sensed Emile's presence. She might hate the female, but that didn't mean she didn't admire her outrageous power.

"What does the emissary want?"

"He said that Emile demands a meeting with you."

"Demands?"

Gideon lifted a slender hand, flinching at the bone-chilling cold in the air. "Her words, not mine."

"Why would I meet with my competitor?"

The vampire shifted from foot to foot, clearly reluctant to reveal what the emissary had told him. Jayla didn't blame him. Jayla had never killed the messenger because she didn't like the message, but there was always a first time for everything.

"Emile claims that she has proof that Dreamscape has been sabotaging her business."

"Sabotage." Jayla repeated the word, trying to make herself accept that she hadn't misheard. Gideon nodded. "What the hell is she talking about?"

Gideon grimaced. "The emissary mentioned busted pipes and food poisoning and a fire in the cloakroom."

"Why would Emile assume I am responsible?"

The male shrugged in confusion, obviously as baffled as she was by the accusations. Jayla was a ruthless assassin, a cunning businesswoman, and a demanding lover. But she possessed one unbreakable moral code rule. She didn't cheat. Ever.

"I don't know, but she is threatening to take her evidence to the clan chief if you refuse to meet with her face-to-face," Gideon warned.

Shit. Jayla pressed her lips together. She was in the process of expanding the resort to include a casino across the river in Macau. This was the last thing she needed.

"Set up an appointment," she snapped.

"The emissary said…" Gideon's words trailed away.

"What?"

"That it had to be now. There's a car waiting."

Was Emile deliberately trying to piss her off? If so, she was doing a brilliant job.

"Fine. But I don't need a chauffeur," Jayla growled. "Send the car away. I'll walk."

The vampire suddenly looked troubled. "Are you sure? I can drive you."

Jayla shook her head. "I want to make sure this isn't a trap."

"Forgive me, mistress, but I really believe—"

"My decision is made." Jayla's expression warned that she was done with the conversation.

Gideon clenched his hands as if battling his urge to argue. Then, with a stiff bow, he backed out of the room.

"Yes, mistress."

* * * *

Azrael had assumed he was prepared for the sight of Jayla. He was wrong.

It was one thing to occasionally have one of his servants check in to make sure she was doing well and in no need of assistance. Quite another to see her in the flesh.

Glorious flesh.

Hidden in a black limo protected by a witch's spell to disguise his scent as well as his thunderous power, he watched as she left the large hotel by a side door and strolled down the street.

Physically, she hadn't changed. Vampires didn't age. Her rich, golden skin glowed in the bright lights from the nearby hotels, and her eyes shimmered like the finest jade. It seemed her preference for fitted satin dresses remained the same. This one was a deep crimson, sleeveless tunic with gold trim. It barely reached her knees, revealing the slender length of her legs and the high, black stilettos that did nothing to hamper her elegant strides.

Tonight, however, her glossy black hair had been left free to tumble down her back. Last time, the elaborate curls had hidden her lethal daggers. Azrael assumed she had them concealed somewhere else.

His body hardened as he allowed himself to fantasize about the various places she might have tucked them out of sight. Next, his mind moved to the pleasure of stripping off that flimsy bit of silk to conduct the treasure hunt.

A growl rumbled in his throat. He'd spent thousands of nights imagining holding this female in his arms. Nibbling her from head to toe and drinking deep of her decadent blood. She'd been a nagging hunger that refused to leave him in peace.

Now, watching her stroll just a few feet away, his entire being was on fire with a savage need to leap out of the car and claim her. *This* was why he'd stayed away. He knew his desire for her would be this intense. This grindingly overwhelming.

It made her too dangerous. He couldn't risk being blinded by a female who'd already killed him once…

"Boss."

The warning voice jerked Azrael out of his bemusement, his head turning toward the driver of the limo.

The vampire was as large as a mountain with a shaved head and dark eyes. He wore leather pants and boots with a white t-shirt that stretched tightly over his bulging muscles. Most people would look at Maxim and assume that he had more brawn than brains. A dangerous mistake.

"What is it?" Azrael demanded.

"She's being followed."

Azrael stiffened, his gaze snapping back toward the window. It was late autumn outside, but the weather was warm with only a slight breeze. This was prime vacation time for Hong Kong, and the streets were jam-packed with tourists.

Leaning forward, Azrael frowned. There. He watched two slender vampires strolling several feet behind Jayla. They might have been sightseers or Dreamscape employees, but there was no missing their hard expressions as they kept careful pace with their prey. Or their matching outfits. Jeans, boots, and red leather jackets. Then, one of the males turned enough for Azrael to catch a glimpse of a small crossbow loaded with a silver bolt clutched in his hand.

Damn.

"Call the others and tell them to do a sweep of the neighborhood," he snapped in terse tones. "Pick up any vampire wearing a red leather jacket."

Maxim reached for his cellphone, glancing over his shoulder. "What do you want me to do?"

"Pull as close to the female as you can get."

Making a quick call to the six clansmen Azrael had brought to the city, Maxim picked up speed, weaving through the heavy traffic before quickly swerving toward the curb. Azrael didn't hesitate, jumping out of the backseat and flowing forward.

He gave Jayla less than a second to sense his approach before dropping a heavy hood over her head and binding her wrists in silver shackles. She briefly struggled, but once he scooped her off her feet to tuck her into the back of the limo, she held herself with a rigid dignity. Like a goddess who was above the stupidity of the world around her.

Azrael frowned as Maxim hit the accelerator and then drove out of the city. Why was Jayla so calm? Had she expected to get kidnapped? Yes, that made sense.

But why set herself up as a target?

He was considering the various options when she impatiently rattled the shackles already searing into her delicate skin. The sound made Azrael flinch. He hated that he was causing her pain, but he couldn't risk allowing her to escape. Not only did he need her, but he also had no idea how many bad guys were lurking in the horde of tourists.

They reached the outskirts of the city, and the car at last pulled into an underground parking lot of a towering apartment building. The limo came to a smooth halt, and opening the car door, Azrael crawled out, gently pulling Jayla behind him. He nodded toward Maxim, and the limo pulled away. Wrapping his arm around her stiff shoulders, he steered Jayla toward a heavy steel door marked with a sign that read: MAINTENANCE.

Placing his hand flat against the door, he used his power to push it open, revealing a narrow flight of stairs. Still holding Jayla close, he headed down to the secret lair. They entered a long, sparsely furnished room with a cement floor, matching walls, and open steel beams above their heads. This was a temporary space for vampires in need of a secure location to stay hidden—or conceal something important.

Azrael needed both.

Leading Jayla toward the small sofa, he pressed on her shoulders until she settled on the edge of the leather cushion. He sat beside her, a potent surge of anticipation tingling through him.

As if sensing his heated gaze that swept over her rigid body, Jayla made a muffled sound of impatience.

"If you intend to kill me, I wish you'd get on with it before I die of boredom."

Azrael smiled with rueful humor. "You haven't lost your arrogance, *kiska*."

She froze at the sound of his voice. Or maybe it was his Russian endearment. She'd reminded him of a hissing cat the first time he'd seen her. Sleek and elegant and utterly lethal. Her rich lotus scent swirling in the air. "Who are you?"

Azrael leaned toward her. "First, I intend to relieve you of any weapons you have hidden beneath that lovely gown."

She hissed in outrage. "Touch me, and I'll kill—"

"Not this time," he interrupted, sweeping his hands down the length of her torso.

It took an effort, but he kept his touch light, refusing to acknowledge the jolts of pleasure racing through him. She was bound and momentarily helpless. He might be a vampire, but he wasn't a monster. Not anymore.

He reached the slender length of her legs when he at last found a sheath tied around her upper thigh. Carefully, he pulled out the slender dagger with its silver blade and tossed it onto a chair across the narrow space. Next, he bent to slide off her shoes, lifting the pointed heels to his nose. Poison. Just as he'd suspected.

"Impressive," he murmured, flipping the shoes to join the dagger. "Now, this." Grabbing the thick hood, he slowly pulled it off her head.

Jayla blinked, a visible tremor racing through her body as she allowed her gaze to skim over his face before lowering to the white cashmere sweater stretched across his chest and then down to his dark slacks.

At last, she slowly shook her head as if coming out of a dream. Or a nightmare.

"No," she rasped. "This is a trick."

"I'm very real," he assured her, leaning forward. She was clearly in shock, but she hadn't panicked. And she hadn't tried to attack. He was willing to take a risk. With quick movements, he unlocked the shackles and let them drop to the floor. Then, he offered her a sensuous smile. "Do you want to touch and prove for yourself?"

Disappointingly, she didn't accept his offer. Instead, she continued staring at him as if he were a ghost.

"You're dead," she breathed.

"We're vampires. Technically, we're both dead."

"I stuck a dagger in your heart and watched you turn to ash."

"True." He reached up to touch the spot where the dagger had slid through his chest. "Thankfully, it takes more than that to put me in my grave." He grimaced. "Or at least it used to."

Her eyes darkened with an emotion he couldn't identify. Disbelief? Regret? Hope? Then, her jaw tightened with rigid resolve.

"I don't know how you managed to create this illusion, but…" Her words died on her lips as Azrael reached into the pocket of his slacks to pull out the jade pendant he'd carried with him for the past seven hundred years.

"Does this help?"

Her ruby lips parted, her gaze locked on the stone. At last, she tilted back her head to study him with a strange expression.

"How?"

"When I was human, someone cursed me by placing my soul in a sword."

Her gaze darted around the barren space, no doubt searching for his weapon. When she didn't find it, she returned her attention to him.

"A witch?" she asked, clearly unperturbed by his revelation.

Of course, she was as old as he was. Over the passage of a thousand years, a creature was bound to have seen or heard most things. Even about crazy-ass curses.

"I'm not sure," he admitted. Vampires had no memory of their lives as humans, and since there'd been no one around to ask when Azrael woke, he hadn't been able to discover who had cursed him. Or why. "But the magic of the sword is fey."

Jayla furrowed her brow as if considering what he'd just revealed. "Does that mean the only way to destroy you is to destroy the sword?"

Azrael hesitated before he nodded. He would be a fool to trust a female who'd already tried to kill him, but then again, he had to rely on her if he were to survive. He needed her, and that meant revealing the truth.

She started to say something, only to snap her lips together as if struck by a sudden thought.

"What is it?" he demanded.

"Did the Anasso know?" She forced the question between stiff lips.

Ah. She was wondering if the brutal king had deliberately tried to send her to her death.

"No." Azrael shook his head. "If he'd discovered I was something other than immortal, he would have stopped at nothing to force me into his clan." His lips twisted into a humorless smile. He'd spent his life virtually alone because he'd known what would happen if he became a weapon for some bloodthirsty master. "What could be better than a trained warrior you can sacrifice over and over in battle?"

She slowly nodded, not revealing if she was comforted by his words or not.

"Is this your revenge?" she abruptly demanded. "Do you intend to kill me?"

"Just the opposite," he assured her. "I intend to offer you a bargain."

Chapter 2

Jayla had once jumped off a cliff on the coast of Ireland to avoid a pack of angry werewolves who'd caught her alone. For endless moments, she'd soared through the air, feeling a strange sense of unreality. It was like flying, only with the knowledge that a devastatingly painful landing awaited at the bottom of the cliff.

That's what it felt like as her hungry gaze drank in the sight of Azrael.

For seven hundred years, she'd mourned the death of this vampire. As if he'd been a vital part of her life and had been ripped away. And worse was the knowledge that she had struck the killing blow. Now, she soared on a dizzying sensation of hope combined with a sickening fear that this was all a hideous trick.

Telling herself that she was searching for some sign of a hoax, she allowed her gaze to roam over Azrael's fiercely beautiful features, silvery hair still cut short, and piercing blue eyes. There were a few differences. He had a large diamond that flashed in his earlobe. She didn't recall it being there during their first meeting. And he wore a sweater that covered his broad chest and the magnificent, winged tattoo on his back. A shame. Really, really a shame.

At last, her gaze settled on the jade pendant dangling from his slender fingers. That wasn't a hoax. It was real, and it was hers. She caught her scent on the fragile necklace. So, who else could have it but Azrael?

Accepting that there was a faint possibility that he was telling the truth, Jayla held tightly to her skepticism. Just like leaping off a cliff with the knowledge she would have a painful landing.

"If you wanted a bargain, you would have approached me at the hotel. There was no need to kidnap me," she pointed out.

His brows lifted, seeming confused by her words. "Kidnapped? Is that what you think happened?"

Was he joking? Her brows snapped together. "I was snatched off the street, blindfolded, and forced to come here against my will. By definition, that's kidnapping."

"You were snatched off the street to rescue you from an ambush, and you were blindfolded because I'm not prepared for you to know the location of my temporary lair," he explained in smooth tones. "You did, after all, kill me the last time our paths crossed."

She flinched at his casual reminder of their previous encounter, but she forced herself to concentrate on his explanation.

"Ambush? What ambush?"

A muffled beep sounded, and Azrael shoved his hand into the pocket of his black slacks to pull out his phone. He glanced at the screen, an expression of satisfaction settling on his lean face.

"Ah. Just in time." He surged to his feet. "Follow me, and I'll answer all your questions."

Jayla frowned, a dark premonition creeping down her spine as she rose and reluctantly followed Azrael out of the room and through a narrow corridor. Absently, she wondered where they were. A bunker? That's what it felt like. Not that it really mattered. If she had to fight her way out, this was as good a spot as any other.

They turned through a maze of hallways, at last stopping at a closed door with a small window cut into the thick steel.

"Have a look," Azrael commanded.

Jayla stepped forward, having to rise on tiptoes to glance through the window. Eye-level for most people was over her head. She didn't know what she expected, but it wasn't a room full of male vampires. Four of them wore red leather jackets and were tied to chairs with silver chains, while six others surrounded the prisoners, their faces grim.

"Do you recognize the vampires in the red jackets?" Azrael demanded.

She studied the males. They each had different hairstyles and features, but the hard, cynical expressions on their faces made them all look alike.

She slowly shook her head. "I've never seen them before. Why?"

"Two of them followed you from Dreamscape," Azrael said. "The other two, my clansmen found just a block from where you were walking, apparently waiting for you to pass by. All of them were carrying crossbows with silver bolts."

Jayla turned toward Azrael, more resigned than shocked by his revelation. "Why were you following me?"

He shrugged. "I was trying to determine the best way to approach you when I realized you were in danger. I called in my clansmen to help sweep up the riffraff."

Her brows arched as she recalled just how easy it'd been for her to sneak into his Moscow lair. Fast forward seven hundred years, and he had guards who'd managed to overpower four armed assassins.

"You've upped your sidekicks," she murmured.

"I learn from my past mistakes."

"I wish I could say the same." Jayla grimaced. She felt battered by the shock of Azrael's return from death, and now the realization that her suspicion that Emile was setting a trap for her was all too real. Suddenly, she wanted to think of anything but the damned female determined to drive Jayla out of Hong Kong. Bitch. "You said that you had a bargain. Tell me what I get out of the deal."

"I assume you would like to know who is responsible for sending four assassins to kill you."

"I already know." He started to frown, but she raised her hand. "What I don't have is the proof I need to convince the clan chief of Hong Kong. Do you?"

"Not yet." He nodded toward the door. "But my superpower is compelling vampires to obey me. I can haul them to the local clan chief and make sure they offer a full confession. It should be all the proof you need."

She was abruptly struck by the distant memory of Azrael's voice echoing through her mind. "I remember. You tried to use it on me."

He gazed down at her, his searing blue eyes sweeping an appreciative gaze over her upturned face.

"You're one of the few capable of defying my commands."

A flutter of pleasure swept through Jayla. She scowled. What was wrong with her? She wasn't a female who fluttered. Not. Ever.

"I'm special."

He stepped toward her, surrounding her in his musk. "Without a doubt."

She savored the raw scent that she'd thought lost forever. "What do you want in return for the information?"

"Your superpower."

Jayla jerked. Damn. Why hadn't she seen that coming? She forced a stiff smile to her lips.

"My talent for brewing the perfect cup of tea?"

"Your ability to stop time."

* * * *

Levet stepped out of a portal and suspiciously sniffed the air. He'd expected to find himself at the bottom of a volcano. Or a sinking iceberg. Vampires had a peculiar sense of humor, and when Chiron, the owner of the Dreamscape Spa and Resort had requested he join him, Levet had assumed that this was yet another opportunity to dump him in some awful location.

Instead, the delicious scents of curry fish-balls and sticky tofu surrounded him. Hmm. Spreading his delicate gold, crimson, and blue wings that should have belonged to a fairy, he patted his rumbling belly. He might be height-challenged for a gargoyle since he barely stood three feet, but he had a full-sized appetite—along with all the appropriate gargoyle features. Stunted horns, a long tail he kept lovingly polished, and gray eyes that matched his skin.

"It *is* Hong Kong," he breathed in appreciation.

A tall, dark-haired male with fine, devilish features glanced down, his brown eyes filled with confusion. "I told you that was where we were going."

"*Oui*, but you also told me that we were going to Monaco for a bachelor party for Basq, and I ended up alone on a desert island. If a sylph hadn't floated past, I might still be stuck there," Levet complained.

The vampire smoothed a hand down the silver jacket of his custom-tailored suit he'd matched with a black silk shirt and gray tie.

"I would never be that lucky," he murmured in dry tones.

Levet ignored him, his gaze darting to the massive Dreamscape Resort that stood directly in front of them. He didn't trust Chiron. Vampire males had a wicked temper and a habit of biting first and asking questions later, but this one did have the most fabulous resorts.

"Are we here to bond?" he demanded, his wings twitching in anticipation. "Do you wish to get a Brazilian wax together?"

"I'd rather have my fangs pulled," Chiron growled.

Levet stuck out his lower lip. "Very well, we can do a mani-pedi, but I insist on champagne. *Dom Perignon.*"

A chill crawled through the warm evening air. "We're not here for a spa day. We're here to find Jayla."

Levet made a sound of disgust. He might have known there would be nothing fun about this latest adventure.

"I do not understand vamp-speak. What is a Jayla?"

"Not a what. A who," Chiron corrected. "The manager of my resort."

"Oh." Levet frowned. "Is she missing?"

"Yes." Chiron pointed toward the side of the towering building constructed of steel and lightly tinted glass. "The last time she was seen, she was leaving through that door."

"When did she disappear?"

"Three hours ago."

Levet sent his companion a puzzled frown. "Three hours? That is it? I have taken showers that last longer than that."

"She's never out of communication with her assistant," Chiron insisted. "And never, ever out of communication with me. If I call, she answers. Simple as that."

Levet shrugged. "She might have lost her phone."

"And there are no other phones in all of Hong Kong?"

The words were sharp, but they didn't disguise the male's apprehension. He truly feared something had happened to his manager.

"There is something else," Levet said.

Chiron reluctantly nodded. "Yes, she was going to meet with a rival resort owner who claimed she was sabotaging her business. Emile demanded they meet immediately."

"A trap?"

Chiron paused as if trying to sort through his inner thoughts. "That's the most obvious explanation," he conceded, his jaw tightening as his fangs peeked between his lips. A visible display of his frustration. "But I'd like to keep my options open. That's why you're here."

"Not for a Brazilian wax?"

"I want you to follow her trail."

Levet wrinkled his snout. "I'm a gargoyle, not a blood dog."

"Bloodhound," Chiron snapped.

Levet sniffed. "Agree to disagree."

Prepared for another snarky response, Levet was caught by surprise when Chiron turned to glance down at him, his expression unnaturally grim.

"Before I was banished, I attempted to convince Tarek that the Anasso was unstable," he told Levet, clearly referring to his days before becoming the leader of the Rebels. "I wasn't as discreet as I should have been, and one of the Anasso's loyal guards decided to keep my mouth shut. Permanently. Jayla saved me from a nasty sneak attack."

"What did she do?" Levet asked, genuinely curious.

"She knocked aside the silver dagger that was thrown at my back and killed the coward." He shook his head as if disgusted with the idea of putting Jayla in such a dangerous situation. "I don't doubt that's why she was banished and forced to become one of the Rebels." His attention returned to Levet. "I owe her."

Levet's wings drooped. He was such a fuc... *Non, non.* Wait. Sucker. *Oui.* That was it. He was such a sucker for a female in danger. Especially one who had proven to possess a kind heart.

He would search for Jayla, but he wouldn't be happy about it.

"And what about what you owe me?" he asked in tart tones.

Chiron shrugged. "Put it on my tab."

"Fah. If you ever pay that tab, I shall be a very rich gargoyle."

"Go do your thing." The vampire waved his hand toward the side door.

"What are you going to do?"

A cold smile touched the vampire's lips. "I want a word with Emile."

Chapter 3

Azrael watched as Jayla's emotions leached from her face as if she were withdrawing deep into herself.

"You're mistaken," she said in cold tones.

Confused by her reaction, Azrael lifted a hand to touch the center of his chest. "I have a scar to prove I'm not mistaken."

"You think I had to cheat to defeat you?"

He swept his gaze over her stoic expression. Why was she trying to deny her amazing ability? Did she fear that he intended for her to use it for some nefarious purpose? He got that. It was the reason he kept his secrets.

"It wasn't cheating," he assured her, wishing he had the right to reach out and touch her. The desire was like a physical ache gnawing at him. "It was a smart tactical decision to win the battle. Why wouldn't you use such a formidable weapon?"

She stubbornly jutted her jaw. "It's not a power I use." Azrael arched his brow, and she made a sound of impatience. "Fine, it's not a power I use anymore."

"Why not?"

"None of your business."

Azrael flinched, not surprised by the stark desire to assure her that everything about her was his business. This was another reason why he'd never allowed himself to get close to her. He'd known exactly what would happen. The scar over his heart burned with regret.

"Since I have need of that particular talent, it is very much my business," he added in smooth tones. "At least, temporarily."

She narrowed her eyes, turning the conversation away from herself. "It is my turn to ask why."

Azrael had known the question was coming, but it was still an effort to force the words past his lips. "My sword has been stolen."

She blinked as if wondering if she'd misheard him. "The sword that contains your soul?"

"That's the one."

"How could you allow it to be stolen?"

Azrael was thousands of years old. He'd traveled the world as a mercenary, killing for profit and acquiring a ruthless reputation along with a massive amount of wealth. He'd indulged in temptation and witnessed unspeakable horror. But for the first time in his very long life, Azrael felt a surge of embarrassment.

"It wasn't really a matter of *allowing* it to be stolen," he muttered.

"Didn't you take precautions to make sure it was safe?"

He clenched his hands in annoyance. Not with Jayla, with himself. Although, there was no need for her to rub salt in the wound.

When he'd awakened to discover the sword missing, he'd been stunned. His first thought had been that he'd misplaced the stupid thing. It wasn't like he constantly carried it around with him. And if he were being honest, after so many eons, he'd grown...careless. There was no other word.

It wasn't until he'd found the note that he realized the true danger.

"No one should have been able to touch it," he told her.

She studied him with open curiosity. "No one?"

"That was my belief," he admitted. "From the moment I woke as a vampire, there has never been anyone who could force themselves to lay a hand on the weapon. I even offered huge sums of money to the demon who could take it from me. It's as if the sword itself repels any hand but mine. That's why I didn't bother to keep it locked away."

"If no one can touch it, then how was it stolen?"

"It would appear that one creature *can* touch the sword," he admitted in harsh tones. "The one who cursed me."

Understanding slowly spread over her face. "The fey."

"Yes."

She considered the implications of his explanation. "Why would they steal it?" she asked the obvious question. "And why now?"

Azrael reached into the pocket of his slacks, pulling up a folded piece of parchment. "The thief left this."

Jayla took the note and lifted it to her nose, her brows arching. "Sage," she murmured in surprise. "A Sylvermyst." She continued sorting through the scents clinging to the parchment. "A male Sylvermyst," she added, sending Azrael a baffled frown. "I thought they fled this world with the dark lord several millennia ago."

The Sylvermyst were fey creatures who'd worshiped the dark lord. They'd not only committed unspeakable evil for their twisted master, but they'd also attempted to enslave other fey.

"A few returned after the dark lord was destroyed," Azrael told her, referring to the epic battle that had occurred a few years ago.

Jayla opened the note, reading the words written in blood. "Revenge delayed, but never forgotten." She lifted her head, her expression still confused. "The creature waited centuries to steal the sword, and that's what he left? It seems...clichéd."

Azrael shrugged. "Sylvermyst were never considered the brightest bulbs in the pack."

She rolled her eyes as he added another cliché. "Are you saying they're a few threads short of a sweater? Fell out of the stupid tree?"

Heat sparked through him at her teasing. Dear goddess, she was a magnificent female. "Exactly."

"Hmm." She tilted her head to the side, her raven hair spilling over her shoulder. "That doesn't explain why you kidnapped me."

"*Rescued* you," he corrected. Jayla eyed him, stubbornly waiting for him to answer her question. "I was convinced no one could steal the sword, but there was always the possibility of it becoming lost. A few centuries ago, I paid a witch to place a locating spell on it."

"So, you did take some precautions," she said in dry tones. "Do you know where it is?"

"A remote cave in the Ural Mountains."

She paused as if waiting for him to continue. "So why didn't you get the sword back?" she finally demanded.

"Because the cave is currently being used by a female dragon who is hatching her egg."

Jayla widened her eyes in shock. "A dragon? In this world?"

Azrael grimaced. She wasn't any more astonished than he'd been when he, at last, tracked down the sword, only to realize that it was in the one place in the entire world he didn't dare enter. As powerful as he might be, he was no match for a female dragon protecting her young.

Especially not when his strength was rapidly draining.

"Like the Sylvermyst, they have returned in small numbers," he told his companion. "And usually only for brief visits."

She slowly nodded, clearly still trying to absorb the knowledge that both Sylvermyst and dragons were back in this world.

"Does that mean the dragon will leave once her egg has hatched?" she asked.

"Possibly."

She lifted her hands. "Then wait until then."

"It could be centuries before the baby dragon hatches out of its shell."

"And?"

"And I will be dead."

She jerked as if his words had caused her physical distress. "Dead-dead?"

He studied her pale face. She seemed genuinely concerned. Did the thought of losing him again trouble her? Or was it a figment of his imagination? He desperately wanted her to...what? Care. Yes. He wanted her to care.

"Dead-dead."

She turned away, her shoulders set at rigid angles. "How long do you have?"

It was a question that plagued him. "Each night, that I'm separated from my sword I'm a little weaker," he told her. "I would guess I have less than a week. Time is ticking. I either face the dragon or wait to die." He felt a fierce stab of fury. "What better revenge for the Sylvermyst who cursed me?"

"Or ask me to stop time so *I* can retrieve the sword," she added in a soft voice.

"Exactly." He hesitated. The next few seconds were the most important of his very long life. "Will you help?"

She turned. Slowly, so slowly. Then, meeting his gaze, she nodded.

"Yes. I'll help."

* * * *

Levet bent toward the ground, following the luscious scent of lotus from Chiron's hotel down the narrow street.

"Do this, Levet," he muttered. "Do that, Levet. Save the world." He clicked his tongue, his demon essence easily allowing him to maneuver through the throng of humans. It wasn't that he was invisible. It was that the mortal mind was *encouraged* not to notice him. "And do I ever get any thanks?" he continued his complaints.

"Do you?" a female asked, her voice light and faintly accented. French?

Coming to an abrupt halt in the shadows of a towering skyrise, Levet turned to regard his unwelcomed companion. She was taller than him but still smaller than most creatures, with a delicate body. She wore a sparkling white cocktail dress and high heels. Her hair was a shade of pale gold and fell in wild spirals to her shoulders. Her eyes were a misty gray, and her skin as pale as frosted snow. She appeared human, but when Levet caught sight of her out of the corner of his eye, he saw the faintest outline of ephemeral wings.

Odd.

"Were you eavesdropping?" he demanded. "It is very rude."

She blinked. "I thought you were talking to me."

"Why would I talk to you?"

"Why wouldn't you?"

Hmm. Good point. He stepped closer, studying her delicate features. He didn't recognize them, but there was something about that voice.

"You seem familiar," he muttered. "Who are you?"

She tilted her head as if confused by the question. "You don't know?"

Levet sniffed the air. Gingersnaps. "Should I?"

"Well, we are family." The female pursed her lips. "But I suppose I can't blame you for not wanting to acknowledge the connection. We are a rather motley crew, even for gargoyles."

"Mötley Crüe?" Levet was more confused than usual. Which was saying something. "The band?"

Now the female looked confused. "What band?"

"Wait. Family?" Levet abruptly realized why her voice was familiar. "Aunt Bertha?"

"Who else would I be?"

Levet allowed his gaze to travel over the sparkly cocktail dress and the delicate heels. The last time he'd seen Bertha, she'd been a seven-foot-tall gargoyle covered in gray skin with leather wings, short horns, and gnarly features covered in moss.

"Why are you in that shape?"

Bertha glanced down, holding out her slim arms as if as confused as Levet by the human body. "I have no idea. I went to sleep on a mountain in Nepal." She shrugged. "I think there was an earthquake. I woke up a century later buried beneath that rubble and in this human shape."

It had been a while since Levet had seen his relative, but that wasn't unusual. He had a firm policy of keeping family reunions to a bare minimum. Preferably zero. Or whatever was less than zero.

"Why do you not change back?"

Bertha dropped her arms, her shoulders slumping. "I don't know how."

Levet studied her in confusion. "Is this a joke?"

"I don't think so. I suppose someone could be playing a trick by sticking me in a human form, but I'm not sure what is amusing about it."

Levet dismissed his aunt's odd appearance. Instead, he concentrated on the fact that she had appeared on this street at the same time as he had. Was it a mere coincidence? Perhaps not. Bertha had occasionally stumbled into his life over the years. Sometimes when he needed her the most, as if fate was taking a hand in directing them to cross paths. Other times, she'd arrived and caused utter chaos. You never knew which you were going to get.

"Why are you in Hong Kong?"

"I'm not really sure." She glanced around in confusion. "I was enjoying a leisurely hike up Mount Everest when I was struck by a sudden compulsion to come here." Her attention returned to Levet. "Did you call for me?"

Did he? Levet scratched his stunted horn. "I do not think so."

"Oh." She flashed a dimpled smile. "Well, I'm here now. What are you doing?"

Levet puffed out his chest. "I'm on a very important mission."

"Are you? How exciting."

Levet parted his lips to lie, only to heave a deep sigh. What was the point? "Not especially."

"But it is important?" Bertha pressed.

"It is important to Chiron," he conceded. "Which means, I must complete my mission before I can return home."

"It sounds as if you will need my help."

"Umm…" Levet cleared his throat, attempting to find the proper way to send his relative on her way. Granted, Bertha was the only family member he liked, but she was notoriously accident-prone. It had been Bertha who'd caused the great fire of London, and while Levet couldn't prove anything, he suspected she might have brought an end to the dinosaurs. "Actually, I'm more of a lone wolf."

She frowned. "Is that what your mother told you?" She tsked. "Dreadful female." She leaned down, speaking slowly. "You're not a wolf. Just a very small gargoyle."

Levet waved his hands in a gesture of impatience. "I mean that I work alone."

"So do I. We should make perfect partners." Bertha pressed her hands together. "What is the mission?"

Levet heaved a sigh. Arguing with Bertha was like trying to teach a vampire manners. Futile.

"I am searching for the manager of the Dreamscape Resort."

"Ah. Is there a reward?"

Levet made a sound of disgust. For the past few years, he'd been an official Knight in Shining Armor, or a KISA as he preferred to be called. Which meant he was constantly being asked to put himself in danger and then tossed aside when his skills were no longer useful.

"There is never a reward."

"Then why are we doing this?"

"I'm not entirely certain," Levet muttered, turning back to the street that was beginning to clear of tourists. It was a reminder that the night was swiftly passing.

It wouldn't be long until dawn arrived, and he would be forced to seek shelter.

"Good enough for me," Bertha fell into step beside him, her barely-there wings fluttering in anticipation. "What does she smell like?"

"Lotus."

Bertha sucked in a deep breath, her eyes widening in surprise. "A vampire." She sniffed again. "A female vampire."

"*Oui.*"

They traced the scent in silence. Levet didn't want to explain how he'd somehow become the minion of a bunch of leeches. Not that he was an actual minion, he silently reassured himself. But…

"Hey, baby." Without warning, three curs appeared in front of them. Curs didn't possess the strength of pureblooded Weres, but they could be dangerous in packs. The largest of the males stepped forward, clearly the alpha. He was over six feet with bulging muscles beneath his too-tight t-shirt and jeans. His head was shaved, and he had a wide leather strap around his neck like a dog collar. He took another step, towering over Bertha. "I'm talking to you."

Bertha glanced around before returning her gaze to the cur. "Me?"

"Yeah, you." The cur shoved his hips forward, pointing toward his crotch. "You want some of this?"

"Okay."

Without warning, Bertha reached out to grab his dangly bits, squeezing hard enough to make the male's eyes cross, and a whimper escape his lips. Then, as if unaware of the damage she inflicted, Bertha twisted the flesh clutched in her hand, sending the male to his knees.

"Hey!"

The two curs standing behind the alpha leaped forward. With a muttered curse, Levet waddled to stand next to his aunt. He couldn't watch her be mauled and not try to help. Could he?

Perhaps sensing his movement, she turned to face him, the translucent wings whacking the charging curs with enough force to send them sprawling flat on their backs.

"Oops." She turned back. "Sorry." She scurried to bend over the closest cur. At the same time, he tried to sit up. Their foreheads smacked together, the sound of the impact echoing like the strike of a gong. The cur groaned, flopping back onto the sidewalk, blood dripping from his busted head. "Sorry," she said again, then turned toward the other cur, holding out her hand. The male whimpered and crab-walked down the sidewalk to escape her assistance.

She glanced back at Levet. "Well, that was rude."

"Perhaps we should go."

Scurrying past the male still on his knees, clutching his crotch in pain, Levet returned to his hunt.

"People claim I am a walking disaster," he muttered with a shake of his head.

"It wasn't my fault," Bertha protested. "He asked if I wanted some of it."

"I do not think he meant for you to yank it off his body."

She shrugged. "He should have been more specific."

"I…" Levet came to a halt, staring at a spot on the sidewalk. "The trail ends here."

Spinning in a slow circle, Levet studied his surroundings. A soaring office building with lots of glass and steel. Next to it, a manicured garden lit by strings of lanterns. Behind him, the main road leading out of the city. It seemed most likely that Jayla had been picked up by a car and driven away.

So how was he supposed to find her now? He was busy debating the question when Bertha reached out to tug his horn.

"Is that vampire a friend of yours?"

Levet jerked away from her grasp. Why were demons forever grabbing his horns? "What vampire?" he asked in grumpy tones.

"The one who is spying on us from behind that tree." Bertha pointed toward the nearby garden. At the same time, there was a blur of darkness as the vampire abruptly took off, heading toward the back of the office building. "There he goes."

"Come on."

Levet flapped his wings, dashing after the fleeing creature. He didn't know if the vampire had anything to do with the missing Jayla, but there had to be a reason he was running away. Besides, he'd just reached a dead end.

He could return to Dreamscape and admit defeat or hope the vampire could give him information.

Levet was a KISA. He never admitted defeat.

Chapter 4

Jayla stepped through a portal created by a pretty fairy. Azrael had hired the fey creature since vampires were incapable of magic, and she'd stared at him with blatant adoration. The gaze bothered Jayla. In truth, it'd taken her considerable willpower not to reach out and slap the female.

Jayla wanted to pretend it was simple frustration. She was, after all, supposed to be meeting with Emile to prevent a potential disaster, not traveling to Siberia to confront a mother dragon who could turn her into a crispy critter with one sneeze. But it wasn't frustration that made her hands curl into tight fists.

It was jealousy.

She didn't want any female looking at Azrael.

Shoving aside the dangerous realization, Jayla glanced around. She'd expected to be standing on top of a mountain. Instead, they were in a deep, thickly wooded valley frosted with a thin layer of ice.

"What are we doing here?" she asked as Azrael appeared beside her.

Dressed in thick leather pants and a heavy sweater, Azrael pointed toward the towering mountain range visible over the trees.

"The cave is on top of that peak."

Jayla tilted back her head. She'd changed, as well. Azrael had provided her with a pair of jeans, a sweatshirt, a heavy parka, and a pair of leather boots. She hadn't asked why he had her precise size. She simply pulled on the warm clothes and braided her hair to keep it out of her face.

"So, why aren't we up there?" she demanded.

"Because the dragon would sense the magic of the portal if it opened in her territory." He grimaced. "We're going to have to sneak up on her while she's sleeping. Slow and careful."

It was a reasonable decision. Jayla had never encountered a dragon, but she knew they were the one creature capable of destroying a vampire with terrifying ease. Slipping in and out of her lair while she slept was no doubt the best plan.

Still, Jayla wasn't excited about the prospect of climbing six thousand feet to reach their destination.

"Are you saying we have to climb up there?"

"Yes."

She considered the distance, then glanced toward the horizon. "Dawn is just a couple of hours away."

"There's a village at the base of the mountain. We can stay at the local lodge," Azrael told her.

They moved through the dense forest, their footsteps crunching on the frosted underbrush. After years of living in a bustling city and surrounded by concrete, Jayla found herself oddly enchanted by the sense of peace that blanketed the remote area. No traffic, no shouts from the street vendors, no blasting sirens. Just the rustle of woodland animals and the silent beauty of the star-speckled sky spread above them.

Or maybe you're enchanted by the male walking close beside you, a voice whispered in the back of her mind.

For endless centuries, she'd imagined what might have happened if she hadn't chosen to kill Azrael that fateful night. What if she'd tossed down her dagger? What if she'd stayed in Moscow?

The potential for what-might-have-been was as painful as the regret for having destroyed a vampire because she refused to see the truth.

Now, she had the opportunity to discover exactly what-if could be. If she dared.

Lost in her thoughts, Jayla suddenly caught the scent of wood smoke. With a blink, she realized they'd stepped into a clearing with a village huddled in the small circle. Reaching behind her back, Jayla made sure her dagger was safely sheathed. She could sense several fey creatures and at least one rock troll.

Azrael didn't hesitate as he walked down a path that led to the center of town. He was obviously comfortable with the area. She wondered how long he'd stayed here, trying to figure out how he could retrieve his sword. The thought of the fear and frustration he must be enduring tugged at Jayla's heart.

Reaching the far end of the street, Azrael halted in front of a large, wooden structure with a steeply slanted roof and a large terrace that offered a stunning view of the nearby mountain range.

Jayla sent Azrael a startled glance as she caught the strange scent of licorice. "A bauk?" she breathed in surprise.

The elusive creatures were small and soft like slugs. They usually hid in deep holes, preferring to avoid other demons.

"A mongrel," Azrael clarified, referring to the fact that the bauk had a mix of demon blood. "Be…"

She sent him a confused glance. "Be what?"

He paused as if considering the appropriate word. "Unthreatening," he said at last. "Siros is a shy creature and is afraid of vampires."

"Smart demon," she murmured, inwardly reassessing how to deal with the upcoming situation.

She might currently be a businesswoman, but she would always be an assassin at heart. That didn't mean using brute strength to achieve her goals. She depended on cunning, finesse, and understanding that each situation was different.

Climbing onto the terrace, they entered the lodge through the front door, crossing the large lobby toward the counter at the back. Jayla swept her gaze over the polished wood floor and paneled walls before tilting back her head to take in the vaulted, open-beamed ceiling. She wasn't interested in architecture. She was just making sure that nothing lurked in the nooks and crannies.

They halted in front of the counter, watching a short, hunchbacked creature with oversized ears and a thatch of brown hair appear from behind a hidden door. He shuffled forward, his shoulders hunched, and his dark eyes darting from side to side as if terrified he was about to be ambushed.

"Hello, Siros."

The male reluctantly glanced toward Azrael, his round face wary. "You."

Azrael shrugged. "Yes, it's me."

"You're back." The creature didn't sound pleased. "Again."

"Obviously. I need a room," Azrael announced.

Siros did more eye darting. "There are other hotels in the area. They are more suited for vampires. Especially if you intend to get into another battle. I demand that this be a place of peace for both me and my customers."

What battle? Jayla arched her brows, but now wasn't the time to ask for details.

"There will be no fighting, I promise you," Azrael assured the male. "Well...well..."

Jayla pasted an apologetic smile on her lips and stepped toward the counter. "It's short notice," she murmured.

"Yes," the male instantly latched on to the ready excuse. "Yes, it is short notice. And I'm very busy."

"I understand," she sympathized, ignoring Azrael's narrowing gaze. She was an expert on the headaches endured by a hotel owner. And how to earn their cooperation. "This is a beautiful lodge. Did you build it yourself?"

Siros's expression remained wary, but he eagerly answered. "My mother did. She's a brownie."

Jayla ran her hand over the smooth counter. She didn't have to pretend her admiration for the wood that had been cut and polished to reveal the lovely grain. This wasn't the prefab stuff used by human builders.

"That explains the beautiful craftsmanship."

The male preened, a faint flush of pleasure staining his cheeks. "Yes. She traveled throughout the world to find the perfect lumber and hand-cut each plank herself." He glanced down as if seeing through the floor. "The foundation was carved from ironstone my mother mined and brought here, piece by piece. We survived three earthquakes that destroyed the other buildings in the village."

"Impressive." Jayla leaned forward, her tone soft. "As a fellow hotelier, I realize this is a terrible imposition, but if you could find space for just one day, I would be forever grateful."

The male grimaced. "One day?"

"One day, I promise." She didn't bat her lashes, but she did give him an inviting smile. "Preferably a sunproof room."

He hesitated. "Perhaps I have something suitable," he grudgingly conceded, refusing to glance in Azrael's direction as he rounded the counter and headed toward a door across the lobby. "Follow me."

Jayla kept a short distance from Siros, just in case there were any unpleasant surprises. She felt the cool rush of Azrael's power as he closed in from behind, protecting her back. She clenched her hands, startled by the intensity of her reaction to his proximity. It was as if having him near made her suddenly realize that her hard-earned independence was no longer enough. An aching awareness that she hungered for a connection that dangled just out of reach.

Jayla followed Siros through the door and down the stone steps to the small cellars, trying to ignore the sensations battering her. The air was cold enough to frost the stone walls and make the floor slick. On the plus side, when the male shoved open a wooden door to reveal their room, it was scrubbed clean with a wide bed and no windows.

"Perfect," Jayla murmured, walking into the shadowed space.

"Is there anything else I can offer?" the demon asked.

"Perhaps blood," Jayla requested. It had been several hours since she'd fed. "Do you have any bottled?"

"I can have it delivered," he assured her.

She reached out to lightly touch his shoulder. "Your generosity won't be forgotten."

The male blushed before turning to scurry back down the hall. Azrael closed the door with a lift of his brows.

"Impressive, but not what I expected from an assassin."

"Brute force has its place, but I prefer diplomacy whenever possible. Not only does it avoid any risk to myself, but when I walk away, I'm not leaving enemies who plot to stab me in the back." She shrugged. "Besides, I'm not an assassin. Not anymore."

The large male leaned against the door, his gaze sliding down her slender body. "Why not?"

Jayla glanced away. It wasn't a question she wanted to answer. "It was time for a career change."

"A career change?"

"Yes."

"It was more than that, wasn't it?" he gently prodded.

Jayla forced herself to meet his searching gaze. "Why do you say that?"

"I know you left the Anasso centuries ago."

Jayla stiffened in surprise. "How?"

"I wasn't spying on you," he assured her as if worried she would be bothered by the idea that she was being secretly stalked. The truth was, the wound deep inside her might have been eased if she could have sensed he was near. "But I did keep track from a distance," he admitted.

"Why?"

The ice-blue eyes darkened, but he didn't explain. Instead, he pressed her for an answer. "Why did you leave the Anasso?"

"I didn't leave," she confessed with a shrug. "I was thrown out."

"Thrown out?" His fangs flashed in outrage. "Are you serious?"

Her lips twitched at his sharp tone. As if he couldn't believe any vampire would be stupid enough to banish her.

"I killed one of his favorite lapdogs."

"That was it?" Azrael's outrage melted to confusion. "Vampires squabble and kill each other on a regular basis. Why did he force you to leave?"

Jayla stared at his sculpted, painfully beautiful face. He wasn't going to let this go. And worse, she sensed that he was as stubborn as she was. Which wasn't easy.

"Fine." She conceded defeat with a scowl. "I refused to use my superpower. Eventually, the king decided that I was no longer worthy of being his personal assassin."

"Ah." Azrael pushed away from the door, gazing down at her with a strange expression. Anticipation? Hunger? Need? Perhaps a combination of all three. "Was there a reason you stopped using your gift?"

She shivered. Not just at the reminder of the damage she'd done in the past, but in reaction to his intoxicating musk.

"It's not a gift. It's a curse," she protested.

He reached out to skim his fingers down her cheek. "As a vampire who's actually been cursed, I can assure you that yours is a gift."

Instinctively, she leaned toward him, craving his touch like a flower sought the sun. "It doesn't feel like it."

"What happened, *kiska*?"

"You." The word was torn from her lips.

Moving slowly as if afraid he might break the spell being woven between them, Azrael grabbed her hand and pressed it to the center of his chest.

"Because of this?"

Jayla splayed her hand, replacing the horrifying memory of slamming the dagger into his heart with the feel of his solid muscles beneath her palm.

"Because I believed you," she admitted, her voice harsh with regret. "I sensed long before I traveled to Moscow that my master was hiding secrets." She grimaced. "And that his lust for personal power had corrupted his desire to unite the vampires."

He lowered his head, wrapping her in his icy power. "And yet you hunted me down?"

She nodded, slowly accepting that she owed him the truth. She had, after all, killed him. He deserved an explanation.

"Before the Anasso discovered me, I was with another clan."

His fingers traced the line of her jaw. "Your voice tells me you weren't happy with them."

Jayla begrudgingly allowed the painful memories to return. The dark, brutal nights, the bloody fights, and the utter emptiness of being treated as an object, never a creature worthy of love.

"I was kept as a prisoner by my master," she told him.

Azrael hissed, his fangs in full view as he pulled back his lips in fury. "You were locked away?"

"Worse," she muttered. "I was leashed like a dog."

"Why?"

It was a question she'd asked night after night as the silver manacle was locked around her neck, and she was dragged behind the other clansmen. It became a running joke to bet on the time it would take for the silver to deplete her strength to the point she fell flat on her face.

"My master made his fortune by taking me from clan to clan to challenge their best fighter for obscene amounts of money."

Ice crawled over the walls as Azrael's anger pulsed through the room. "I assume they looked at your…" His gaze traveled down her slender body. "Delectably compact size and thought you would be easy to overpower."

"Yes."

"How did you escape?"

A grim smile curved her lips. "I didn't," she admitted. She would always regret that she hadn't found the courage to destroy her sire. "One night, the Anasso was passing and watched the battle."

"Did he witness you using your power?"

Jayla nodded. She'd just destroyed a mongrel troll who'd nearly taken off her head with his heavy club, and her sire was collecting his winnings when she caught sight of a huge vampire surrounded by his guards. There'd been no mistaking the shattering power that had surrounded him or the hunger in his eyes.

"I'm not sure how he realized what'd happened since he should have been unaware of time stopping," she told Azrael. "But as we were leaving with our winnings, he appeared in our path. Before I knew what was happening, my master was dead." Jayla had been weary from the battle and in pain from the silver manacle that had been cinched around her neck, so she hadn't noticed the small earthquakes that'd signaled the approach of the unknown vampire. It wasn't until she watched her sire being jerked backwards and then crumbling to the ground that she realized her nightmare was over. "A few minutes later, I was leaving with the Anasso." She met Azrael's gaze, willing him to understand why she'd been so loyal to a male who'd manipulated and lied to her. "For the first time in my existence, I felt safe."

He frowned. "He turned you into an assassin."

"I was in control of my own destiny," she insisted. Nothing had ever felt so glorious as to know she could freely move around the lair and be a welcomed member of the clan. Plus, there'd been something intoxicating about the knowledge that she was a favorite of the Anasso. She grimaced. Eventually, things had changed. An unseen rot had slowly moved through the clan, infecting all of them. "At least, in the beginning."

"And now?"

A genuine smile curved her lips. The best decision she'd ever made was leaving with Chiron and the other Rebels. Or at least, it'd been the best decision until a few hours ago.

It was yet to be seen how her decision to help Azrael would turn out.

"I have an independence I never dreamed possible."

"Ah." His features tightened as he dropped his hand and stepped back.

Jayla frowned, not sure why she could sense that her words wounded Azrael. Or why she was so troubled by the thought that she might have hurt him.

"How did you become a mercenary?" she asked, eager to change the conversation.

He hesitated as if lost in his thoughts. Then, with a shake of his head, he returned his attention to her.

"Unlike you, I was blessed with a sire who considered me her son," he said.

"Did she know that you were cursed?"

"Yes, but she didn't know how it'd happened or why," he shrugged. "I stayed with Bea and our small clan for centuries."

Jayla frowned. She'd sensed a darkness when she first saw him in

Moscow. As if he'd suffered a tragedy. That was one of the reasons she'd felt drawn to him. It was odd to think she'd been so wrong.

"Why did you leave her?" she asked.

"I didn't." He turned to the side, revealing the feathered tattoo that crawled down the length of his neck. Jayla had a fierce urge to reach up and trace the delicate lines. "One night, we were attacked by a rival clan." Ice crawled over the walls, revealing that Azrael was battling a powerful emotion. "Within hours, we were all slaughtered."

She studied his tightly clenched profile. "But you lived."

"Yes. When I woke, I found my clan dead and our homes destroyed."

Jayla resisted the urge to wrap her arms around him. She had been right. He *had* suffered a tragedy. It must have been horrifying to wake and realize that your family was dead. He'd not only had to deal with his grief but also the guilt of having survived.

"I'm sorry," she murmured.

"I made a decision at that moment that I would travel the world alone."

It explained how he'd become a mercenary. A lone vampire would have to possess the skills to protect themselves as well as earn a living. Few actually enjoyed hiding in caves and scrounging dinner from passing hikers. They desired a safe lair and at least a few comforts. Now, however, Jayla had a new question.

"You said when you kidnapped me—"

"*Rescued*," he corrected.

She didn't argue. "You said that you sent your clansmen to capture the vampires following me," she reminded him. "So, you're no longer alone."

"True." He slowly turned, his expression brooding as he gazed down at her. "Seven hundred years ago, I realized that I craved a family." He placed a hand over his unbeating heart. "In fact, it was driven home with painful clarity."

Her lips parted, but before she could speak, a loud knock sounded on the door.

"Dinner!" Siros called out.

Chapter 5

Chiron strolled into the lobby of the hotel several blocks from Dreamscape. It was the first time he'd stepped foot into the rival resort.

Not surprisingly, it was as large as his and equally sophisticated. What he didn't expect was the dramatic black and gold décor. His brows arched as his gaze ran over the sleek furnishings: supple black leather and steel-framed tables with smoky black glass. The floors were a polished black marble, and in each corner stood a massive, priceless vase in isolated glory.

It reeked of sex appeal. Expensive, addictive sex appeal.

Chiron was busy considering the practicality of discovering the interior decorator responsible for the design to update Dreamscape when a female vampire appeared in front of him.

She was young, at least in vampire years, with blond hair pulled into a smooth knot at the back of her head. She wore a black A-line skirt and a shimmering gold blouse. The smile pasted to her lips revealed a hint of fang.

"Come with me."

Chiron tilted his head. He hadn't been trying to sneak in. He was too powerful not to alert every demon in the area that he was there. But he didn't appreciate the female's tone.

"What if I don't want to?"

Lifting her hand, the female held Chiron's gaze as three large vampires in black uniforms stepped out of the shadows. They looked like clones. All bald, each packed with muscle, and all staring at him in hopes he'd give them an excuse to beat the shit out of him.

Chiron hesitated. He wasn't a male who allowed other creatures to intimidate him. He did the intimidating. And he did it very well. But he was genuinely concerned for Jayla. If it meant indulging Emile's need to flex her muscles, then so be it.

"Lead the way."

The female swiveled on her high heels and led him through a side door into a narrow hallway. Distantly, he heard the sounds of the kitchen staff as they prepared for the humans who would soon be lining up at the breakfast buffet. They turned into another hallway that ended at a private elevator. The female pulled out a small card and touched it to the control panel. The gold-plated doors slid open, and she gestured for Chiron to enter.

Hesitating for only a few seconds, Chiron stepped into the elevator and watched the panels close, locking him in the six-by-six space. If this were a trap, he'd deal with whatever waited for him. If worse came to worst, he'd left word with Styx before entering the hotel. The King of Vampires would come searching if Chiron didn't check in by dawn.

There was a woosh, and Chiron plummeted downward. Like most vampires, Emile obviously preferred to control her empire from below. Underground was the only place guaranteed to be sunproof. The doors slid open, and Chiron stepped into a vast office that reflected the décor from above. Black marble floors, gold walls, and streamlined furnishings.

The female vampire matched her theme.

A tall and proud demon with stunningly beautiful features, she had long, deep gold hair and eyes as black as a midnight sky. She wore a black silk pantsuit with a long jacket that plunged to a deep vee, revealing that she had nothing underneath but smooth, pale skin. Her heels were three inches and shimmered gold in the muted light.

"Chiron. I'm honored." The female folded her arms over her chest. "I would have been more honored if you'd sent word you planned to visit."

"And ruin the surprise?" Chiron drawled, closely studying the female. Her expression was impossible to read.

"I don't like surprises."

Chiron decided for a direct attack. "I don't like the fact that my manager has disappeared."

"Manager? What manager?"

"Jayla."

Emile stood as still as death, her dark eyes narrowing. "Is this some sort of riddle?"

Chiron stepped forward, attempting to use his powers to peek into her thoughts. There was nothing. She was too powerful.

"You tell me," he said, forced to determine if she was telling the truth by using his other senses.

Emile clicked her tongue. "The height of the tourist season is not the best time to play games, Chiron. Perhaps you could return..." She lifted her arm to look at the Rolex strapped around her slender wrist. "Never."

Chiron wasn't amused. "If you believe this is a game, Emile, you're going to be very, very sorry."

The scent of black dahlias swirled through the air, the only indication the female was at the end of her patience.

"Tell me why you're here."

Chiron allowed her to see his exasperation. He should be in Vegas in the arms of his mate, not engaged in a stare-down with this female.

"I told you. Jayla is missing."

"You're serious?"

"Always."

"Why would you assume that I have any idea where she might be?"

Chiron frowned. Either this female was really oblivious to Jayla's disappearance, or she was the best actress he'd ever encountered. It annoyed the hell out of him that he couldn't be sure which one.

"Since you were the one who demanded a meeting with her, you're the obvious choice."

"Demanded a meeting?" Genuine surprise flared through the midnight eyes. "Why would I want to meet with Jayla? We aren't exactly BFFs. In fact, the last time we crossed paths, she threatened to carve out my heart and eat it for dinner."

Chiron hissed. He'd charged into the hotel, fully expecting the female to lie to him. But he hadn't expected to believe her. Now, he felt as if someone were trying to yank a rug from beneath his feet. He didn't like it.

"Your emissary passed along your accusations."

"Emissary. What emissary?"

"The one who accused Dreamscape of sabotaging your hotel. He also warned that you intended to take your complaints to the clan chief if Jayla didn't agree to come to your office and discuss the crimes immediately."

Puzzlement visibly changed to anger as Emile lowered her arms, her hands clutched into tight fists. At last. An emotion.

"This is bullshit," she snapped. "If you believe you can make up nasty lies to ruin my reputation, you are sadly mistaken."

A thick, icy mist formed in the room, revealing the female's hidden talent. She could no doubt create a blinding fog if she needed.

"Why would I want to ruin your reputation?"

"To convince the clan chief to shut down my business." She waved a hand around her elegant office. "It's obviously thriving."

"As is Dreamscape."

She extended her fangs, her fury vibrating through the air. "I don't have to cheat to win."

Shit. Chiron got a quick peek into her mind as she struggled to control her temper. She had no idea where Jayla was or who had taken his clanswoman.

"You didn't send an emissary." It was a statement, not a question.

"No."

"You didn't make accusations of sabotage."

She pursed her lips. "If I thought Jayla was attempting to destroy my hotel, I wouldn't have sent an emissary to confront her. I would have come myself."

Chiron spun away, trying to imagine what had happened. "So, who would have pretended to be speaking for you?"

"Only someone very stupid. Or with a death wish."

He nodded. The room pulsed with her frigid power. She wasn't a vampire he'd want to take on in a head-to-head battle.

"It had to be a trap for Jayla," he muttered in absent tones. "Why else create such an elaborate ruse to get her out of the hotel?"

"Or for you," Emile countered.

He turned back to meet her dark gaze. "What do you mean?"

"You've acquired a number of enemies over the centuries."

Chiron shrugged. He hated to brag, but his list of enemies *was* impressively long. "I try."

She looked as if she were resisting the urge to roll her eyes. "They would be fools to attempt to attack you in your own lair."

He followed her logic. "So they kidnapped Jayla to lure me to Hong Kong."

"It worked, didn't it?"

"Possibly," he slowly agreed, a whisper of unease making him hesitate. It was the most logical conclusion, yet... "No," he abruptly burst out, hit with a sudden realization.

"You have another theory?" Emile demanded.

"They could have kidnapped Jayla without involving you," he pointed out.

"True."

"But making me believe you were behind her disappearance was guaranteed to cause trouble between us." He recalled the large vampires with bad attitudes who'd been in the lobby. "Perhaps even a war."

Emile blinked. "Who would want that?"

"Who wouldn't?"

* * * *

Levet ignored the nearby building's open door. It was a red heifer. *Non*. Wait. That wasn't right. A red herring. *Oui*. A red herring.

The vampire they were chasing had pretended to duck through the door, but Levet could sense the creature beneath their feet. Bending low, he moved along the alleyway. At last finding the small grate set in the ground, he pulled it off.

Bertha bent down beside him, her nose wrinkling. "You're certain he went down there?"

"*Oui*," Levet assured her, not giving himself time to consider the possibility that it was a trap.

He'd discovered that assuming that something great was about to happen made life much nicer. Could there be a clan of rabid bloodsuckers waiting to do terrible things to him? Possibly. But it was also possible that a K-Pop group used the tunnels to hide from their rabid fans, was it not?

Dropping through the opening, Levet landed on the hard cement far below. He grimaced, holding his wings off the damp ground as he glanced around the massive tunnel. Thankfully, they used it for drainage and not sewage, but it was still dark and dank and boring. A long tube of cement with cement pillars and occasional ventilation shafts. Why couldn't the vampire have hidden in a nearby resort? Perhaps in the kitchens, where there would be platters of roast goose and fried rice and hot, braised abalone. Mmm. His stomach rumbled.

Bertha landed lightly beside him, the air stirring as she used her invisible wings to break her fall. "I smell him," she announced with a sparkle in her eyes. "This way."

She darted off before Levet could halt her, and he was forced to scramble to keep up. It was annoying. He should be the one recklessly charging into danger. She was stealing his swagger. Rude.

"Wait," he warned as he caught the sound of voices. "The leech is near. And he is not alone."

Together, they pressed against the cement wall and inched toward the side tunnel just ahead.

"Escaped?" The voice was muffled as if they were behind a closed door. "What the hell are you talking about? You promised she would be dead before dawn."

Levet leaned toward the opening of the tunnel, struggling to hear the conversation.

"We were just a block away from the ambush we'd set up when a car stopped, and a vampire grabbed her off the street and drove away," a second voice said.

Levet arched his brows. He'd assumed he was following whoever had snatched Jayla. Instead, it appeared the vamps had intended to ambush her, but someone had gotten to her first.

"Why didn't you follow, you incompetent idiot?" voice one demanded.

"We were attacked."

"Attacked? By who?"

"I don't know. They were vampires, but they weren't local. I've never seen them before."

Levet exchanged a glance with Bertha. Why would strange vampires travel to Hong Kong to kidnap Jayla just seconds before she was to be ambushed and killed? Even among the convoluted vampire politics, it seemed…convoluted.

"What happened?" voice one snapped.

"After the female was snatched off the street, a half-dozen vampires swarmed out of the shadows and grabbed my brothers. There was nothing we could do." Even though it was almost impossible to make out the words, Levet could smell the tinge of irritation in the air. It smelled like charcoal.

There was a long silence as if the first vampire was considering the ramifications of Jayla's kidnapping.

"She must have been warned," the voice said at last. "One of your crew is a traitor."

"Impossible. If she discovered the plan, then it didn't come from us."

"You would say that, wouldn't you?"

The scent of charcoal disappeared only to be replaced by... Levet wrinkled his snout. It wasn't fear. Unease.

"What do you mean?"

"You were the only one not captured by the mysterious vampires," vampire one pointed out.

"I told you, I was monitoring the situation from the gardens."

A layer of ice coated the cement walls. One or both of the vampires was pissed off. Levet was betting on both.

"Tell me about the vampire who took Jayla."

"I don't know. He was big, blond hair." There was a pause. "I think he had something tattooed on his neck."

"That's it?"

"I only got a quick glance."

There was another layer of ice, and this one crawled over Levet and Bertha, coating them in frost. Levet flapped his wings, getting rid of it.

"What about the car?" It was vamp one again.

"A big, black limo."

"And?"

"And that's it."

Levet flinched. He wasn't the most perceptive creature. Hard to believe, but with all his other skills, there was bound to be one talent that was less than awesome. But even he knew that was a terrible answer.

"Either you betrayed me or you're completely incompetent." Vamp one was barely speaking over a whisper. Levet took a step down the side tunnel, straining to hear. "It doesn't matter which one it is. I no longer need you."

"Wait..." Levet didn't need to strain to hear the shrill scream of fear. It came through loud and clear. "No, we had a deal."

"Consider it canceled."

Levet hissed as the presence of the second vampire simply disappeared. Poof. He was gone.

"Umm." Bertha took a step backward at the sound of a door being pulled open. "I think it's time to leave."

"Good idea," Levet muttered.

The click of leather soles against cement echoed through the tunnel, and Bertha reached out to grab Levet by the wing, dragging him farther down the main tunnel.

"Let's leave faster."

Levet clicked his tongue. Had she seen his legs? They weren't built for speed. "I am going as fast as I can," he protested.

There was a blast of icy air from behind. Levet didn't turn his head. He assumed the vampire had caught sight of them and was now hot on their trail.

"This way." Bertha tugged him into one of the side passages.

They sprinted through the darkness, attempting to stay ahead of the pursuing vampire. But just as Levet dared to hope they might avoid a painful death, a solid cement wall appeared ahead of them.

"Uh-oh," he muttered. "Dead end."

Turning to discover if they had time to escape, Levet searched for their pursuer. There was nothing. Just a thick, empty darkness. Was it possible they had shaken the vampire? Just as he dared to hope it was possible, he heard a dull, ominous thud overhead. As if someone above them had dropped something. Something really, really heavy. Like the Eiffel Tower. Seconds later, the ceiling began to form fissures that spread from side to side. Dust filled the air, and the fissures widened to cracks. The next thing Levet knew, the cement turned to rubble.

"Well, this is a bummer," Bertha said a second before the ceiling collapsed on their heads.

Chapter 6

Mere seconds after the sun slid over the horizon, Azrael led Jayla out of the hotel and toward the nearby mountain.

He wasn't only in a hurry to get his sword back—although that was high on the list. But it'd also been nothing less than torture spending hours alone with the glorious female. The fierce desire to take her in his arms and claim her had slammed through him with the force of a tornado. It was only the knowledge that he wasn't certain that Jayla's power could retrieve his sword that leashed his instincts.

Even if Jayla was prepared to become his mate—and that was still a big *if*—he wouldn't burden her with a male who would be dead within a few weeks. If not days. Once he had the sword in his hands, he would devote the rest of eternity to convincing her that they belonged together.

Glancing over his shoulder, he watched as Jayla pushed her way through the heavy underbrush.

"Do you know where you're going?" she demanded, obviously not enjoying her scuffle with Mother Nature.

"I found a trail the first time I tried to get into the cave," he assured her, leaping onto a tall boulder and then moving onto the ledge that wound its way up the steep incline.

Jayla quickly walked at his side. The path was narrow, but vampires possessed an uncanny grace and balance.

"How close did you get?" she asked, tilting back her head to study the peek far above them.

"To the edge of the ridge." Azrael pointed toward the crest just below the cave. "Then, a blast of fire nearly ended everything. If I hadn't taken a dive off the side of the mountain, I would be ash."

His tone was light, but at the time, he'd felt a sharp-edged terror. For his very long existence, he'd been beyond immortal. He'd become accustomed to taking risks with no worry of consequences. The realization that he would no longer return from the dead without his sword, combined with his weakened condition, had forced Azrael to confront his impending death with blinding clarity.

He'd realized what was important. Or, more importantly, precisely *who* was important.

"Ah, that explains the battle Siros was talking about," she murmured.

Azrael frowned before he recalled the manager whining about his extended stay when he'd crawled back to the hotel, broken and bloody from his fall.

"I didn't want to confess that I'd been fleeing from a dragon," he admitted. "Siros would never have let me through the door."

Jayla sent him a wry glance. "Was it when you were diving off the mountain that you decided to invite me to confront a hormonal dragon protecting her egg?"

"After the fall, I had a couple of long and painful days of healing to consider my options," he admitted. "That's when I decided to approach you."

There were a few minutes of silence as they tackled the steepest section of the path, the loose rocks beneath their feet threatening their balance. It wasn't until they rounded a bend that she asked the question that had seemingly been on her mind.

"Why not before then?"

"Besides the fact that you tried to kill me the last time our paths crossed?" he teased.

She studied him with a searching gaze as if his answer was important to her. "Is that really the reason you stayed away?"

Azrael reached up to touch the jade pendant he wore around his neck. It'd been there since he'd awakened in his Moscow lair to discover it lying on the floor beside him. At the time, he'd told himself that it was a reminder not to be distracted by a pretty face, but he'd known even then that it had nothing to do with Jayla's beauty. He'd clung to the pendant as if it were a talisman. A tangible connection to a future he desperately desired.

"No." His voice was as soft as the snow that drifted from the low-hanging clouds. "You know why."

"Do I?"

He arched his brows. "Are you going to pretend that you didn't sense the connection between us?" He slowed his pace, willing her to speak the truth. It didn't matter that he'd possibly chosen the worst time and place for this conversation. Or that he'd promised himself he wouldn't press Jayla until after they'd retrieved his sword. He needed to hear her confess that there was something special between them. "It felt as if I'd been struck by lightning," he murmured, accepting that if he expected her to share her feelings, he would have to do the same. "Why do you think I tried to convince you to leave? I didn't want to fight you."

She glanced away, the sweet scent of lotus filling the air. "And that's why I stabbed you through the heart. You terrified me."

Azrael jerked, startled by her confession. Afraid of him? "Because of my ability to touch the minds of demons?"

"No." She glanced back at him, her eyes narrowed. "Although I might stab you again if you try to meddle with my thoughts."

Relief blasted through him at her teasing. More than a few demons resented his ability to compel them. If Jayla had truly been frightened by his talent, it would have been...unbearable.

"It doesn't have to be a bad thing," he assured her, his voice low and husky. "I can give you pleasure beyond your wildest dreams without even touching you."

Her eyes darkened, awareness heating the frigid night air. She even started to sway in his direction when she abruptly jerked away.

"I still don't understand why you stayed away," she muttered, picking up her speed as they followed the path that twisted sharply upward.

Azrael's long strides easily kept pace beside her, his gaze locked on her rigid profile. "Because I knew if I sought you out and we were together again, I would never walk away."

Her hands clenched into tight fists. "And you didn't want to be with me?"

Azrael muttered a curse. Not want to be with her? There'd been nights when the hunger to seek her out had been nothing short of torture.

"If you knew how I struggled to stay away," he rasped, pointing toward the edge of the path that plummeted toward the unforgiving rocks far below. "It was worse than leaping off this damned mountain."

She kept her face averted, but Azrael could sense a portion of her tension ease. "Then why?"

"I told myself it was because I'm cursed." He shrugged. "What female would want to be with a male who has no memory of the awful deeds he committed? Besides, there was always the chance that the curse might someday consume me."

"But that wasn't the reason?"

"Not entirely." He narrowed his eyes as a punishing wind whipped over the top of the mountain, threatening to lift them off the path and into the abyss.

Was it reminding him that this wasn't the time or place for the conversation? Leaning forward, he braced himself as they reached the upper ridge.

"Are you going to tell me?" Jayla demanded.

He glanced to where she walked at his side. She moved easily up the path, her slender form far more aerodynamic than his bulk.

"You're very stubborn," he helpfully pointed out.

"It's my finest quality."

His lips twisted as he ran a slow, thorough gaze down the length of her slender curves. "Not even close."

"Azrael."

It was Azrael's turn to glance away. He'd spent the majority of his existence as a ruthless mercenary. It was the only way to survive on his own. There'd never been any need to share his emotions.

"I mourned my clan for a thousand years," he told her, grimacing as a dull throb spread through his chest as the image of a slender female vampire with silver-blond hair and blue eyes seared through his mind. She hadn't been a mother. Vampires didn't have traditional parents. But she'd cared for him and taught him how to survive, which was more than most vampires were offered. Her death had left a gaping hole in his life. "I still mourn them," he admitted. "How could I survive if I lost a mate?"

She jerked as if she'd taken a physical blow. "Mate?"

Azrael shrugged. He couldn't tell if she was pleased or terrified by his confession. Maybe both. "You did demand an explanation."

She shook her head. "You couldn't know for certain. We spent less than ten minutes together." She sent him a wry glance. "And those minutes were spent with you trying to convince me that my master was a lying, manipulative bastard while I was trying to kill you."

Azrael smiled. She had a point. "It might not have been the most romantic first meeting, but that doesn't alter the fact that I recognized you as my mate the moment you entered my lair," he insisted. "I wasn't going to risk becoming more deeply connected to you."

"Until your life depended on it," she said, the soft words nearly lost on the fierce breeze.

"I'll admit that it gave me the excuse I needed," he told her. "But I'd already started to accept that I didn't want to be alone anymore."

She slowed her pace, sending him a curious glance. "Is that why you started your clan?"

Azrael released a wry chuckle. "Actually, I didn't start it. At least, not in the beginning."

"They just appeared?" she asked dryly.

"Sort of," he agreed. "A local clan chief in Copenhagen paid me to deal with a vampire who'd made a deal with an ogre tribe to destroy him. After I dispatched the renegade vampire, I found a dozen vampires locked in his dungeons." He shrugged. "I wasn't going to leave them imprisoned, so I opened their cell doors and released them. The last thing I expected was for them to follow me when I left."

Her lips twitched as if she were amused at the image of him returning to his lair with a dozen vampires trailing behind him like lost puppies. He hadn't been nearly so amused. At least, not at the time. He'd tried to run them off, but they refused to go more than a few miles from his lair. They insisted they were in his debt for him releasing them from the dungeon. And no matter how many times he told them he didn't need repayment, they refused to budge.

At last, he'd given in to the inevitable.

"I slowly allowed myself to accept my need for family," he murmured. "I also accepted that being away from you caused more pain than I was avoiding. At some point, I knew I'd need to search for you. I wouldn't have been able to stop myself." He paused, waiting for her to respond. When she remained silent, he reached out to brush his finger down her cheek. "It's your turn."

"My turn for what?"

"Why did I terrify you?"

She easily leaped over a large boulder blocking the path. "You made me question my devotion to my master," she said. "I wasn't prepared to accept the truth."

"And that's it?" he pressed. "Just a fear of realizing you were being manipulated?"

"There might have been more." Each word sounded as if it were being wrenched from her lips.

Azrael stepped close to her side as the path narrowed. "Why do I sense you would prefer to confront the dragon than reveal your feelings?"

"It would certainly be less awkward," she muttered.

"Why is it awkward?"

"I'm not a touchy-feely sort of vampire. I don't discuss my..."

Azrael hid his smile as her words trailed away. He preferred not to endure another dagger strike to his heart. At least, not until he got his sword back.

"Emotions?"

"Exactly."

"Why not?"

Her jaw tightened. "I have a talent for killing and business."

"And for charming demons," he added. Siros had been bewitched.

"But I have no talent for sharing my feelings."

Azrael resisted the urge to tease her. They were the same. Although she'd been with a clan, she was a loner by nature. It meant that neither of them was a lovey-dovey vampire. They knew how to hunt, kill, and escape. They would never spend their nights curled up on a couch, reciting poetry to each other.

And he was okay with that.

"If you find words difficult, I'm not opposed to you demonstrating your emotions in other ways," he offered, his voice low and husky.

She sent him a wry smile. "So generous."

"True," he agreed. "I'm renowned for my generosity."

A silence descended as they approached a towering rock formation directly in front of them. The ridge that led to the cave was just on the other side.

"I didn't want you to die," Jayla abruptly confessed.

If Azrael had a heart that beat, it would have stopped at her words. The words he'd waited seven hundred years to hear. Still, he ached for more.

"Because?"

"Because it destroyed a part of me."

"There. That wasn't so hard, was it?" he teased.

"I'd rather face the dragon," she groused, climbing over the jagged rock with graceful ease.

Azrael quickly followed behind her, grimacing at the shocking heat that smacked him directly in the face.

"You're about to get your opportunity," he said, a shudder racing through him.

He hadn't forgotten the sensation of being this close to a dragon, but he'd told himself that his memory was an exaggeration. After all, nothing like a near-death experience got the adrenaline pumping. Even for a vampire.

Beside him, Jayla held out her hand as if astonished by the thick air that pulsed against them. "It feels like we've entered the netherworld."

Azrael nodded toward the nearby cave. "It only gets worse."

Coming to an abrupt halt, Jayla turned to face him. "You stay here."

Before he realized what he intended to do, Azrael reached out to grasp her arm. "Jayla."

She sent him a puzzled frown. "I'll return before you know it. Literally."

He tightened his grip, unwilling to let her go. "Not yet."

"The longer we wait, the more danger to both of us."

She was right. They were close enough that the dragon would sense them if she woke. So why wasn't he urging her to hurry and retrieve his sword?

Because he was suddenly terrified, he realized with a jolt of surprise. It was easy to concoct the daring plan when he was tucked in his bed, recovering from his injuries. He'd get Jayla up the mountain, and she could stop time and retrieve the sword. In and out. No fuss, no muss, right? Now, standing on the ridge with the savage power threatening to crush them, he couldn't release his hold on her.

The thought of allowing her to waltz into the den of a dragon…no, not just a dragon, a female dragon protecting her egg…twisted his gut into a knot of sheer terror.

"Are you certain your power will work on a dragon?" he demanded.

She arched her brows as if caught off guard by the question. "There's only one way to find out."

"No." Still holding her arm, he pulled her back toward the rock that blocked the path. "I should never have asked you to come here."

Jayla dug in her heels. "What are you doing?"

"I can't allow you to enter that cave," he announced, his voice hard with regret. Why the hell had he ever brought her to this place? "Not when we have no idea if the dragon is immune to your powers. Or even if you'll be able to hold onto the sword."

"Without your sword, you'll die."

He glanced away from her hauntingly beautiful face, watching the snowflakes drift past and swirl down the chasm just a few inches away.

"Perhaps it's my fate," he murmured in soft tones. "I have risen from the grave more times than a vampire has any right to—"

"No." Without warning, Jayla reached up to frame his face in her hands. "A miracle brought you back into my life. Nothing is going to take you away again."

He felt the cool brush of her lips.

Then the world froze.

Chapter 7

Jayla took a dangerous minute to simply savor the sight of Azrael frozen by her powers. Like an exquisite butterfly suspended in amber. The last time he'd been trapped, she'd stuck a dagger in his heart. Now, she allowed her gaze to trace the perfect lines of his face and the brilliant blue of his eyes.

This astonishing male had not only forgiven her for killing him, but he was convinced that she was his mate.

And she agreed.

Jayla had known he was special from the moment she'd caught his wild, fiercely male scent. It had settled deep in her heart, haunting her dreams for the past seven hundred years. A part of her had accepted that she'd destroyed her mate. And the fact that she was destined to be eternally alone.

It seemed a fitting punishment.

Now…

A perilous hope bloomed in the very center of her being. As Azrael had said, they didn't have the most romantic beginning, but that didn't mean they couldn't have a romantic ending. Right?

But only if you retrieve the sword, a voice in the back of her mind urgently reminded her.

Spinning on her heel, Jayla dashed toward the nearby cave. The heat in the air remained, but it no longer pulsed with an unspoken threat. Snowflakes hovered in mid-air like miniature stars.

It'd been so long since she'd used her power, she had almost forgotten the sheer beauty of a world standing utterly still. Not that she would linger to appreciate the sight. Her power burned through her with alarming speed. It wouldn't be long before it completely drained her.

Moving with blinding speed, Jayla entered the dragon's den. She had a vague impression of a massive form curled at the very back of the cave, along with piles of bones from the animals—and a few demons—she'd been chomping on to ease her hunger. Closer to the front was a scattering of coins, jewels, and uncut gems. No doubt they were offerings from the locals.

Everyone knew the best way to appease a dragon was to add to their hoard.

Among the treasures, Jayla spotted a dozen weapons. Only one, however, wasn't encrusted with diamonds or rubies or emeralds.

It was the sword she'd seen Azrael holding when they were in Moscow.

Darting forward, Jayla grabbed the weapon, never slowing as she dashed out of the cave and along the narrow ridge. She had only seconds before her power faded, and time started ticking again. She wanted to put as much distance as possible between her and the dragon before the lethal creature caught her scent.

She was a few feet away from Azrael when her power started to sputter. She could see her companion's fingers begin to twitch, but before he opened his eyes, the scent of herbs swirled through the air.

Coming to a halt, Jayla glanced over her shoulder. Nothing. It wasn't until a shadow passed over her head that she realized a creature had been perched on a jagged peak above the ridge.

She clutched the sword in her hand, barely possessing the strength to stand upright, let alone fight. And, worse, as time started flowing again, she felt an unpleasant sensation in the palm of her hand. As if the sword were waking up and trying to escape.

The creature landed lightly on the path, directly between her and Azrael.

"Who are you?" he demanded, his arrogant tones rasping against Jayla's raw nerves.

She squared her shoulders, sweeping a disdainful gaze over the intruder. He was obviously fey with delicate features and a slender body covered by leather pants and a matching jacket. It wasn't until she caught sight of his strangely metallic bronze eyes that matched his long hair that she realized he was one of the rare Sylvermyst.

An evil fey. And most certainly the male who had cursed Azrael.

Why else would he be in this remote area? It couldn't be a coincidence.

Jayla twirled the sword, pretending the leather hilt wasn't sending jagged pain through the palm of her hand and up her arm. She would have only a couple of minutes before holding the weapon became unbearable.

"I'm Jayla." Her tones were even more arrogant. "Who are you?"

He narrowed his odd eyes, keeping a wary distance between them as the frigid temperature dropped to sub-zero. He wasn't stupid.

"I'm Silvanus. The owner of that sword you're holding."

Jayla had centuries of practice keeping her expression a polite mask as she sent a glance toward Azrael. Dealing with humans demanded the patience of a saint. Still, she struggled to hide her confusion as the male vampire stood frozen in place. Had he somehow been injured by her powers? Then Jayla watched as he slowly closed one eye. A wink. Ah. Belatedly, she realized that he was pretending to be immobile to fool the Sylvermyst.

Jayla returned her attention to Silvanus. "This sword?" she asked, giving it another twirl.

"That one. It belongs to me."

"Strange," she drawled. "The vampire standing behind you seems to think it belongs to him. He offered me a treasure chest filled with gems to retrieve it."

Silvanus risked a glance over his shoulder to make sure Azrael wasn't sneaking up on him. Once he was confident that the vampire didn't pose a threat, he swiveled his head back to study Jayla with a tight smile.

"I'm curious. How did you manage to get it out of the cave?"

"I put the dragon to sleep," she easily lied.

"How?"

She shrugged. "It's my superpower."

"Amazing." There was genuine admiration in his tone. There should be. Only a shitload of power could actually put a dragon to sleep. "So, why is the vampire standing like a statue?"

"I used my power on him, as well."

"Why?"

Jayla shrugged again. "When he approached me to retrieve the sword, he offered me a fortune before we ever started negotiations. It made me start to think that there must be something very special about the weapon. And if he would pay that much, there must be others out there who would pay even more."

He blinked as if shocked by her explanation. "You double-crossed a fellow vampire?"

"Business is business."

A slow, evil smile curved his lips. "I like your style."

Jayla stepped toward him, her eyes narrowed. "You're not going to like it when I kick your ass over the side of this mountain."

"No need for violence."

"Then move out of my way."

His smile faded, a hint of fear darkening his bronzed eyes. "Not until you give me the sword."

She flashed her fully extended fangs, taking another step forward. "Never. Going. To. Happen."

He lifted his hands in a gesture of peace. "Wait." He swallowed hard as if he had a lump in his throat. "It's worthless," he forced himself to admit at last.

"What?"

"The sword." He nodded toward the weapon. "It has no monetary value."

She hissed. "Do you think I'm stupid? The vampire wouldn't have offered a treasure chest of gems if it was worthless."

"He needs the sword because he's cursed."

She frowned in pretend confusion, waving the sword in a gesture that forced the fey to take a quick step backward. She wanted space in case the male decided to try and physically take the weapon from her.

"What's a curse got to do with this?"

"His soul is bound to it."

She held the sword in front of her face as if inspecting it for some sign of the soul. "You did that?"

"Yes."

"Why?"

The male's jaw tightened. He didn't want to answer. Then again, he knew he couldn't overpower her.

"When he was human, his Viking ship landed near my tribal land," he muttered.

She clicked her tongue in impatience, hoping the Sylvermyst couldn't detect the shudders of agony that had started to vibrate through her body. The sword was doing everything in its power to escape.

"And? A mortal couldn't hurt a Sylvermyst. Even if he was a

Viking."

"No, but he could plunder and destroy the village of the local humans."

"So?"

The snow was picking up, falling from the clouds in thick swirls of white. Within the blink of an eye, the path was covered in a frozen layer.

"Those humans were our slaves. Not to mention, they provided females for our harems," Silvanus complained. "He had no right to destroy them."

Jayla frowned, genuinely puzzled by the fey's petulance. It wasn't uncommon for demons to consider humans their personal servants or to choose them to warm their beds. But one human was as good as another. Why did he take these humans' deaths so personally? And why Azrael.

"Surely, he didn't do all the plundering," she pointed out, keeping her tone casual. She didn't want him to realize the importance of his answer. "Did you curse the others?"

"Azrael was the leader, and his reputation preceded him." The male's lips twisted. "The Angel of Death."

"Angel of Death?" she repeated, recalling her first encounter with Azrael.

There'd been something…lethal about him. Even when he'd tried to avoid fighting her, she'd known that he could destroy her with terrifying ease. That's why she'd used her power. But since he'd arrived in Hong Kong, there'd been something different about him.

Oh, he wasn't harmless. Far from it. But he'd lost the brutal edge of a mercenary. Just as she'd lost an assassin's ability to kill without mercy.

"That's what people called him," Silvanus said, his voice harsh with anger. "He even had wings tattooed on his back to help spread the rumors. He enjoyed the fear that rippled through the lands."

Jayla abruptly realized why this male had cursed Azrael. It wasn't about him pillaging the humans or destroying his harem.

Silvanus was jealous.

Azrael had obviously been a legend in his time. A fearsome warrior who'd spread terror throughout the lands. The Sylvermyst had been just another evil fey who would never have songs written about him or cause nightmares among the natives. He was a dull, petty creature.

It might have been funny if it hadn't nearly caused Azrael's tragic end.

"So, you decided to punish him?" she forced herself to ask, sending a glance toward Azrael.

They had the information on why he had been cursed. It was time to get rid of the disgusting creature.

Unaware of his impending death, Silvanus smirked at the memory of cursing his enemy.

"Yes. And it had to be a punishment that would last for an eternity." The smirk faded as his eyes flashed with frustration. "I planned to use the sword to torment him, but before I could have my fun, I was forced to leave this world."

"Now you're back to take your revenge?"

"Exactly. I want to watch that bastard suffer. And I finally have my opportunity." He held out his hand. "Give me the sword."

Jayla settled her features into a bored expression as if she were over the desire to fight for the weapon. "You really want it?"

The fey stepped toward her, anticipation smoldering in his eyes. "Yes."

"Very well."

With a movement too fast to anticipate, Jayla lifted the sword and threw it end over end. At the same time, Azrael flowed forward, snatching the blade out of the air and swinging it in a wide arc. Silvanus turned, his hands desperately reaching out as if he could wrestle the weapon from Azrael's hands.

In his panic, Silvanus didn't even bother to duck as the blade swung toward him, slicing through his neck.

Grimacing, Jayla watched the male's head fly off his body, bouncing down the side of the abyss. At the same time there was a loud popping sound as the curse was broken.

"Done," Azrael said, tossing the sword over the edge of the cliff with a grim smile of satisfaction.

* * * *

For Azrael, the journey back to the lodge at the base of the mountain was a blur of icy wind and blinding snow as they gingerly made their way down the treacherous path. He'd been struggling to accept that the curse was well and truly broken, not to mention the strange sensation of having his soul nestled back into the center of his being.

It was a lot to process.

Back in the village, however, his confrontation with Siros was vividly burned into his mind. The bauk demon had been dead set against letting them stay another day. Quite literally. Azrael had threatened to rip out his heart and feed it to the dragon with no luck. Jayla offering an exhausted smile and a soft plea for assistance had finally induced the male to begrudgingly lead them back to the room in the cellar.

At last alone, Azrael closed the door and leaned down to pull off his heavy, snow-coated boots. Next, he removed his thick sweater, now damp and clinging unpleasantly to his skin, before moving to help Jayla slip off her boots and heavy parka. At first, he'd assumed he was keeping busy to avoid thinking about Silvanus and the reason he'd been cursed. He wasn't proud of the thought that he'd spent his human years slaughtering helpless villagers. But as he slowly straightened to gaze down at Jayla's pale, perfect face, he knew that wasn't the reason.

The Viking he'd been in the past had been destroyed when his sire turned him into a vampire. No. He was trying to keep himself from tossing Jayla onto the bed. It didn't matter that she was weary from using her powers to retrieve his sword or probably frozen to the bone after their journey through the howling blizzard. His body, his heart and soul, ached to hold her in his arms.

Jayla tilted back her head to regard him with a small smile. "Siros is going to bar the doors the next time he sees us coming."

"Doubtful," he said dryly. "He's enchanted by you. As am I."

She blinked. "Enchanted?"

He nodded without hesitation. "Enchanted. Enthralled. Obsessed."

Slowly, she lifted her hands to place them against his bare chest. "At least you're no longer cursed."

Wrapping his arms around her narrow waist, Azrael splayed his hands against her lower back.

"Thanks to you," he murmured. "Not only did you retrieve my sword, but you also kept Silvanus distracted."

"You were the one to strike the killing blow," she reminded him, arching her body forward. "You freed yourself."

Azrael released a low growl. Silvanus was dead, but the memory of what he'd done to him would never be forgotten.

"No doubt I deserved to be cursed," he admitted. "But I'm glad it's gone."

"Even though you won't be returning from the grave?" she teased.

His hands lowered to cup her ass, desperate to feel her pressed tight against his thickening cock.

"My reckless days as a mercenary are over. I intend to retire and live a very quiet, peaceful eternity with my exquisite mate."

He braced himself for her to pull away. Or at least to deny that she was his mate. Instead, she smoothed her palms over his upper chest.

"I suppose I could use some muscle at Dreamscape," she murmured.

Azrael shuddered. Her light touch set him on fire. As if they stood in the dragon's den, not in the lodge's icy cellar. A primitive hunger spread through him. It craved more than sex. Or blood. It wanted her heart and soul, for all eternity.

He slowly lowered his head. "I have muscles."

"Do you?" she muttered, tilting back her head as he nibbled his way down her throat.

"Do you need proof?"

She chuckled softly. "I insist on inspecting the merchandise for myself."

"Go for it," he encouraged, ready and willing to be inspected— preferably with her tongue and fangs.

Her fingers continued exploring the ridges and planes of his chest when she suddenly stiffened.

"My pendant."

Azrael lifted his head to discover her staring at the jade amulet tied around his throat. "Mine," he corrected in firm tones. "You gave it to me."

She traced the smooth jade, her expression one of remorse. "I regretted what I'd done the moment my dagger entered your heart." Her fingers moved to touch the scar in the center of his chest. "If I could have taken it back, I would have. I left this necklace because it was a reminder to me that freedom has its own price."

He bent his head to sweep his lips over her furrowed brow. "Fate occasionally has a wicked sense of humor. It brought us together as enemies—"

"Never enemies," she sharply interrupted.

His lips skimmed down her cheek to nuzzle at the corner of her lips. "What about your mate?"

He could feel her tension ease as she snuggled close. "There's a possibility I could be convinced."

Relief scorched through him, nearly sending him to his knees. Until that second, he'd been terrified to hope that she would agree to become his.

"A possibility?" He kept his tone light. He didn't want to scare her away with the sheer force of his need.

"Mmm." She scraped her nails down his chest hard enough to draw blood. Azrael trembled as the pleasurable jolts zigzagged through him. Sex was great. Sex with bites, scratches, and screams of bliss was paradise. "I'm a very demanding female. You can ask my employees at the resort."

He slowly narrowed his gaze at her teasing words. It was a direct challenge. Hell, yeah. He was ready and willing to convince this female that he was the male she needed in her bed. The *only* male she needed.

Sliding his hands beneath her sweatshirt, he tugged it over her head and tossed it aside. The sight of her lacy bra with its ruby studded clip between her breasts wrenched a wicked chuckle from his throat. It was as delicate and sexy as she was.

"So how do you want to be convinced?" he murmured. He lowered his head to scrape the tip of his fang along the line of her collarbone.

She trembled, her hands sliding up his chest to grasp his shoulders. "That's a start."

"You are demanding," he chided, carefully peeling off her bra before cupping her breasts in his palms.

The scent of lotus perfumed the air as she wrapped her arms around his neck. "And hungry."

"For this?" He brushed his thumbs over her nipples.

Her eyes darkened with excitement. "Yes."

"And this?" His head lowered, his lips closing over the tip of her breast.

She hissed, her body arching in pleasure. "Yes."

"There's more."

Using the tip of his tongue to tease her nipple to a hard peak, Azrael expertly attacked the fastening to her jeans. He swiftly had them wiggled down her legs, along with her frilly undies.

Once she was naked, he scooped her off her feet and headed to the bed. Laying her on the narrow mattress, he peeled off his slacks and joined her. Pulling her into his arms, he kissed her with a desperate hunger.

"More, more, more," she murmured when he finally allowed her to speak.

"I've spent seven hundred years fantasizing about touching you." His hands skimmed the curves of her back, savored the softness of her skin.

"I'm no fantasy," she assured him.

"Thank the goddess," he rasped, cupping her ass.

"Azrael," she whispered.

"You're as soft as silk."

She pressed against him, her lips skimming down the length of his jaw. "You're hard as steel."

"And getting harder by the second," he assured her.

With a low chuckle, she reached down to wrap her fingers around his full arousal. "So I noticed."

Desire clawed deep inside him. He wanted this female. He wanted to take her fast and furiously, with his fangs buried deep in her throat. Pagan passion at its best. Then he wanted a slow, delicious seduction that would last hours. Perhaps days. When he was done, he wanted to start all over again.

First, however, he wanted to know that their futures were bound together. "Are you prepared to complete the mating?"

She held his gaze, her expression calm. "It's the one thing I'm sure of," she assured him. "You belong to me."

Azrael moved to frame her face in his hands. "For all eternity." Leaning forward, he kissed her with an aching need.

Jayla melted toward him. "For eternity."

Unable to wait another moment, Azrael cupped the back of her head and tilted it to the side. Hunger slammed through him at the exposed length of her slender neck, a feast for his senses.

His fangs lengthened, his cock twitching in anticipation.

"My beautiful assassin," he whispered before striking with blurring speed. Jayla jerked as his fangs sank deep into her silken flesh. But not in pain. The intoxicating scent of lotus drenched the air and hit his tongue as he drank deeply of her blood. "Mine," he rasped, feeling the shocking power of the mating bond explode through him.

Removing his fangs, he tenderly licked the tiny puncture wounds, a searing heat crawling beneath the skin of his forearm as the mating mark slowly appeared. The elaborate crimson tattoo would be a visible statement that he was well and truly mated.

To the most exquisite female in the world.

* * * *

Jayla's body trembled as a raw, primitive need tore through her. She'd felt desire and hunger, but nothing like this. It was savage. As if she'd be ripped apart if she didn't sate the demands of her body.

Immediately.

With a low growl, Jayla pressed her hands against Azrael's shoulders, and with one fierce push, had Azrael flipped onto his back. Not giving him time to react, she rolled on top of him, straddling his hips and gazing down at him with smug satisfaction.

Not that he appeared to mind their new positions. In fact, Azrael's eyes smoldered with anticipation as he reached up to span her waist with his hands.

"I should have known you would want to be on top," he murmured in a husky voice.

She lowered her head to trail her lips over his shoulders, relishing the sense of empowerment that flowed through her blood. Azrael was a formidable warrior who had no need to constantly puff up his ego. He knew he could destroy anything in his path, so it didn't bother him to surrender control.

"Are you saying I'm bossy?" she teased, using the tip of her tongue to circle his flat nipple.

He muttered his pleasure in a low growl, his fingers digging into her flesh. "On occasion."

"Is that a problem?" she whispered, moving steadily lower.

"We can take turns," he rasped.

"Deal." She nibbled a slow path of kisses down his torso.

"Jayla," he choked as she reached the rigid muscles of his lower stomach.

"Hmm?"

"Even vampires have limits," he ground out.

She gave a throaty chuckle as she deliberately rubbed back up the length of his body. Her nerves sizzled with awareness, sensitized to the point of near pain.

"Limits are meant to be tested."

"Consider me tested." Without warning, he slid his hands down to grasp her hips, arching off the mattress to press the fierce jut of his erection against her. Jayla moaned, the aching desire becoming a sharp, ruthless need as the tip of him slipped just inside. "Make me yours, *kiska*."

"Yes."

She pulled back her lips, revealing her razor-sharp fangs, then used one tip to score a deep furrow next to the scar her dagger had left. Holding his smoldering gaze, she lapped the rich blood that filled the wound.

An unexpected concussion of electricity rippled through Jayla. As if she'd just been struck by lightning. Fate was clearly a badass female who didn't want a silly vampire to miss the fact that she'd just been eternally mated. And Jayla was totally fine with that.

"Mine," she whispered, feeling the mating mark sizzle beneath the skin of her forearm.

"Yours."

Azrael lifted his head off the mattress, claiming her lips with a searing act of possession. Then, spreading kisses over her face, he stroked his lips down the length of her neck. Jayla dug her fingers into his shoulders as he relentlessly tugged her upward.

"Azrael…" Her words faltered as he caught the hardened tip of her breast between his teeth. Her head fell back as he tugged and suckled her, the insistent pleasure crashing through her. He moved to the other breast, ruthlessly driving her passions to the point of no return.

She wanted him inside her. She wanted his erection driving so deep that neither would know where one started and the other ended. But even as she widened her legs to allow his cock inside her, he pulled her up his body.

She moaned as his mouth teased a path down her stomach, occasionally scraping a fang against her shivering flesh. Then, gripping her hips tightly in his hands, he positioned her directly over his head. Jayla planted her hands flat against the cold wall as his mouth found her moist cleft.

She squeezed her eyes shut, struggling not to melt into a puddle of pure bliss as his tongue reached out to stroke the highly sensitive flesh. It was deliciously decadent to be poised above him as he expertly urged her toward the looming climax.

Wallowing in erotic sensations, she allowed him to pleasure her. He located the pinpoint center of her pleasure with torturous care, keeping her steady with a steely grip.

Jayla clenched her fangs as he gently stoked the building fire inside her, completely lost in the blazing delight. It was nearly too late when she abruptly pulled away from his magical touch.

"Wait, Azrael…" she gasped.

Easily sensing she wanted him deep inside her when she came, Azrael guided her back down his body, positioning her so that he could slowly penetrate her softness. Jayla released a harsh sigh of relief as she pushed herself against his hard cock. Nothing had ever felt so right.

Taking a moment to savor the sense of utter completion, she finally opened her eyes when Azrael lay unmoving beneath her. Her lethal Siberian tiger crouched and ready to pounce.

"Azrael?" she asked in puzzlement.

"Your turn to be the boss, Jayla," he rasped.

A slow smile of delight curved her lips as she placed her hands flat on his chest and lifted her hips before sliding back down with enough force to make him grunt in mindless bliss.

Azrael growled, his eyes shimmering with an ancient contentment. "Maybe I should worry that I can't come back from the grave," he teased. "I'm fairly certain you're going to kill me. Again."

In answer, Jayla pulled up and slammed down. Then she lifted herself higher before plunging downward again. His hips arched off the mattress, his lips pulled back to reveal fully extended fangs. Jayla moaned with heady satisfaction, thoroughly enjoying having this male at her mercy.

He belonged to her. For all eternity.

Their souls were bound together. Their unbeating hearts entangled to the point where his every emotion was nestled deep inside her. As if they truly were one.

Slowly, deliberately, she drove them both to the edge of frenzy, waiting until he pleaded for mercy before pumping against him with blinding speed.

Azrael shouted her name at the same moment she violently convulsed around him, his body trembling beneath her. Holding herself still, Jayla savored the sensations pulsing through her. The feel of Azrael lying beneath her, the delicious throbbing of her orgasm, the tingle of her brand-new mating mark. If she could use her power to capture this perfect moment in time, she would.

Instead, she collapsed against him in utter exhaustion.

Chapter 8

Levet glared up at Bertha, who currently stood on his shoulders as she dug through the pile of rubble above them. It'd been hours since they'd been buried in the tunnel, and he was over this current adventure. There was nothing fun about being trapped, coated in a thick layer of dust, with his aunt digging her heels into the tender muscles of his neck.

He was going to give Chiron a very stern lecture about luring him to Hong Kong. This was not the exotic, fun-filled getaway Levet had been promised.

"Stand still," Bertha chided, sending a shower of pebbles bouncing off Levet's head as she pushed against a large boulder.

Levet coughed, wiggling his wings as the grit threatened to wedge into the delicate nooks and crannies. And his wings weren't the only nooks and crannies getting wedged with grit.

"I do not know why I must be the one on the bottom," he complained.

"Because my arms are longer," she told him, grunting as she continued to shove at the boulder. "I'm the only one who can dig us out."

"Oh." Levet furrowed his brow, sensing there was something fishy about her argument. "Wait—"

"I'm through!" There was the sound of stone cracking and another cloud of dust before the pressure on his shoulders abruptly disappeared. Levet tilted back his head to see a narrow hole that Bertha had busted open. Her head appeared in the space, her expression smug. Clearly, she was pleased with her success. "Do you need help?"

Levet scowled. He was a hero. Of course, he did not need assistance. "Stand aside," he commanded.

Flapping his wings, he managed to lift himself off the ground and through the cramped hole, landing awkwardly next to his aunt. He flushed, grabbing his tail to give it a good polish. He wasn't meant to fly. He was a gargoyle, not a stupid bird. Still, it was embarrassing to flounder around like a bloated turkey.

"I could have gotten us out much faster if you'd allowed me to use my magic," he complained.

Bertha easily scrambled over the broken cement, leading him back to the main tunnel. "I love you, nephew, but I'm not willing to spend the next century recovering from your fireballs."

Levet clicked his tongue. "I have very fine balls."

"They're a disaster."

"Hey…" Levet allowed his protest to die away. It wasn't that he wasn't confident his balls were the finest in the land, but he'd been distracted by a sudden smell.

Bending low, he waddled toward the end of the tunnel before using the iron rungs in the cement wall to climb up and out of the drainage system. He halted as he glanced around the small garden next to a towering hotel. The dark streets were beginning to fill with tourists, but he ignored the frenzied chaos. It wasn't so easy to ignore the aroma of the street vendors.

Mmm…

Bertha moved to stand next to him. "Levet?"

He shook his head, dismissing his gnawing hunger. He'd get a snack later. Like a full roasted pig. And pie. Apple pie.

"I smell the vampire," he told his companion.

Bertha arched her brows. "The one who trapped us?"

"*Oui.* But it is odd."

"What's odd?"

Levet nodded toward the nearby hotel. "This is the resort where Jayla works."

Bertha's expression was distracted as she considered the various possibilities. "The first ambush was a bust," she finally said. "Perhaps they're hoping a second will be more successful."

Levet nodded. Bertha was right. "And they would know this is the place she would return. Let's go."

Pumping his feet as fast as they would go, Levet headed out of the garden and circled the edge of the pool. Then, using a side door, he darted into the front lobby. He was just about to track down the treacherous vampire when a chill blasted through the air, and a towering form abruptly blocked his path.

"Levet," Chiron snapped. "Where the hell have you been?" The vampire's icy gaze turned toward Bertha as she halted next to Levet. "And who is this?"

Levet slammed his hands on his hips. He was filthy, hungry, and in a M.O.O.D. "I have been buried beneath a ton of rubbish, thanks to you," he snapped. "And this is my Aunt Bertha."

Chiron stilled, whether shocked by Levet's tone or his explanation was impossible to guess. "Are you joking?"

Levet clicked his tongue. "I was following Jayla's trail when Aunt Bertha appeared—"

"She's related to you?" Chiron interrupted.

"Of course. She is my mother's sister." Levet glanced toward the delicate woman standing next to him. "Can you not see the resemblance?"

"No."

Bertha sent Chiron a sour glare. "Rude."

"Right?" Levet demanded. "Vampires."

Chiron clenched his hands into tight fists as if struggling to keep from strangling Levet. "What about Jayla?"

"I was about to tell you when you interrupted," Levet complained.

Ice coated the marble floor. "Levet."

Levet wisely stepped back, sensing he'd pressed the vampire far enough. Leeches were notoriously short-tempered.

"We halted at the spot where Jayla was kidnapped."

Chiron stared down at him, his face tight with impatience. "Kidnapped? Who kidnapped her?"

"Some vampire with blond hair," Levet repeated the words he'd overheard. "Not a local."

"In a black limo," Bertha helpfully added.

Chiron glanced down at the tips of his polished shoes as if wishing he was a million miles away. Finally, he returned his attention to Levet.

"Did you see her being kidnapped?"

"*Non*, we followed the vampire who witnessed it."

"Where is he?"

"Dead. Killed by the same vampire who collapsed a ceiling on our heads." Levet held up his hands to reveal his cracked claws. "It took hours to dig out and totally ruined my manicure. You owe me."

Chiron rolled his eyes. "You give me a headache."

Levet flapped his wings. "The feeling is entirely mutual."

"I…" The vampire's words trailed away as his gaze moved toward the double glass doors at the front of the lobby. "Jayla."

Without warning, a roar ripped from the male's throat, and he raced across the marble floor, moving so fast he was a blur of darkness. Unaware of what was happening, the clusters of guests still sensed the violence throbbing in the frigid air, their screams echoing through the lobby as they fled in terror.

* * * *

Jayla was lovesick.

There was no other explanation for the goofy smile that refused to leave her face, or the way she kept reaching out to touch Azrael as they walked through the doors of the Dreamscape Resort. As if she were afraid that he might be a figment of her fevered imagination and would disappear without warning. It would take a century or ten to accept that the glorious male was truly her mate.

It also explained why she failed to notice the very large vampire barreling across the lobby, headed directly for them.

It wasn't until Azrael released a low growl and stepped in front of her that she recognized the danger. Well, that, and the screams as her guests scattered throughout the lobby.

"Chiron. Stop." Moving with blinding speed, Jayla pushed past Azrael and held her hands out, determined to stop the charging vampire before he could inflict any damage. "What are you doing?"

With obvious reluctance, Chiron came to an abrupt halt, glaring at Azrael. "Is this the bastard who kidnapped you?"

"No." Jayla grimaced, realizing she wasn't being entirely honest. "Well…yes, but he's my mate."

Chiron's eyes widened in shock. "Mate?"

She nodded. "Azrael." She smiled as Azrael placed a protective arm around her shoulders. Glancing toward his grim expression, she wrapped her arm around his waist. Violence still throbbed in the air. One wrong move, and there would be bloodshed. "This is Chiron. My employer. And friend." She waited for Azrael to offer a grudging nod before turning her head to meet Chiron's frigid gaze. "What are you doing here?"

"You disappeared, so I came looking for you."

"As did I."

Jayla jerked in surprise as a tiny creature with oversized wings waddled around Chiron. At first, she thought it must be a mongrel fairy, then she caught sight of the gargoyle features and stunted horns.

"You must be Levet," she murmured, trying to hide her smile. She'd heard enough rumors about the miniature gargoyle to recognize him.

Levet offered a sweeping bow. "Knight in Shining Armor, at your service."

Chiron muttered something about chunks of granite and bottom of Victoria Harbour before giving a sharp shake of his head.

"What happened?" he asked Jayla.

Jayla's felt her fangs lengthen. She'd been putting off the troubles waiting for her in Hong Kong to simply savor her new mate. Reluctantly, she accepted that it was time to face the devil.

"Emile," she snapped. "The bitch set an ambush for me. If it hadn't been for Azrael, I would be dead."

Chiron was shaking his head before she finished speaking. "It wasn't Emile."

Jayla blinked in confusion. "You're sure?"

"Positive."

She didn't doubt him. Chiron had obviously managed to peek into Emile's mind to be so certain. "Then who?"

"That vampire," the gargoyle abruptly interrupted, pointing toward a red-haired male who'd just entered the lobby to glance around in confusion at the stampede of humans. "He paid mercenaries to destroy you."

Gideon.

Shock momentarily held Jayla frozen in place, then she sent a warning glare toward the two males next to her.

"He's mine," she growled, hurtling across the lobby before Gideon realized the danger. Grabbing him by the throat, Jayla slammed the slender male against the wall.

"Bastard," she rasped, not sure if she was more hurt or infuriated by the male's treachery.

Hazel eyes widened in horror before he belatedly attempted to cover his ass. "Jayla. Where have you been? I was so worried—"

"Why?" she snarled, interrupting his lame attempt at innocence. "I saved you. If it hadn't been for me, you would still be in the slave pens. And you betray me?"

The pretense dropped away to reveal the stark craving just below the surface. "Did you think I would be your pet employee forever?" Gideon sneered, his handsome face twisted into an ugly expression. "I have my own ambitions."

"What ambitions?"

"To own a resort." He spat the words like a curse.

Jayla shook her head, sickened to realize how easily this male had fooled her. Why hadn't she sensed his greed? Or his willingness to destroy her to fulfill his goal?

"No one was keeping you here. You could have walked away if you wanted to start a business," she snapped.

Gideon glanced over her shoulder at the vast, elegant lobby. "I wanted this one."

Jayla furrowed her brow in confusion. "You thought Chiron would give it to you?"

"He intended to start a war between Emile and me," Chiron clarified as he and Azrael strolled over to stand next to her.

"Why?"

"So the clan chief would ban us from Hong Kong." Chiron sent Gideon a jaundiced glare. "Obviously, he assumed he could take over the resort once we were gone."

"Coward," she hissed in disgust. There was no worse insult among vampires.

Azrael lightly brushed his fingers down the curve of her spine. "Do you want him dead?"

Jayla considered. Killing the bastard would certainly solve her problems. But it wasn't enough. She'd been an assassin for long enough to know there were many things worse than death.

"No. I want him to suffer."

Chiron arched a brow. "Torture?"

She shook her head, a slow smile spreading across her face. "He can spend the rest of eternity scrubbing dishes and taking out the trash." She released her grip on Gideon to lean against her mate. The feel of him strong and steady helped to banish the aching sense of betrayal. "While he envies our happiness."

Gideon hissed, his pride revolted at the thought of being reduced to menial labor. Especially when he would be performing that labor for mere humans. "Just kill me."

Chiron reached out to grab the male by the back of his neck, easily lifting him off the floor. "He can start now."

Jayla watched as Chiron hauled the squirming vampire out of the lobby. She didn't doubt that her master would take some time to personally punish Gideon, but for now, she didn't want to think about the traitor.

Instead, she turned to wrap her arms around Azrael, laying her head against the center of his chest.

"It's over."

He dropped a kiss on top of her head. "I'm pleased to know you can still stick a knife in the heart when necessary, *kiska*," he teased, referring to Gideon's horror at spending the rest of eternity with his hands stuck in a kitchen sink.

"You were showing a few of your mercenary skills yourself, Angel of Death," she murmured, recalling his swift impulse to protect her from Chiron.

He wrapped her tightly in his arms as if he never intended to let her go. "Clearly, we were destined for one another."

Jayla closed her eyes, absorbing the wild, masculine scent that filled her senses. "Clearly."

Epilogue

Hong Kong
Three weeks later…

Azrael finished his sweep of the main casino, making sure that the large crowd of human tourists was happily spending vast sums of money before heading toward the side exit. He'd taken over the role as head of security at the new Dreamscape Resort and Casino, replacing the old guards with his vampires. They had no way of knowing if Gideon had managed to corrupt any other employees, and Azrael wasn't willing to take any risks.

Not when it came to his beloved mate.

A smile touched his lips as he pushed open the glass door and stepped into the side garden. His life had gone from being a marauding Viking known as the Angel of Death, to a cursed recluse, to a security guard at a casino in Hong Kong.

And he couldn't be happier.

Jayla had enriched his existence in ways he couldn't even put into words. It was as if he'd existed in a dull world of black and white that had suddenly exploded with luscious colors and tastes and joy. Lots and lots of joy.

The tantalizing scent of lotus teased his nose, and Azrael stepped into the sunken patio to discover his mate standing in the shadows of a large hibiscus. She'd asked him to join her, but he had no idea why.

Crossing the flagstones, Azrael allowed his gaze to sweep down her slender body wrapped in his favorite crimson tunic. Or, at least, it was a duplicate of his favorite tunic, he wryly conceded. Jayla had started to order them by the crate-load since they'd been mated. He had a habit of ripping them off her whenever they had a moment alone.

Which wasn't nearly often enough as far as he was concerned.

His lips parted to ask what she was doing, only to be distracted when she pointed toward the center of the patio with a mysterious smile. Turning his head, Azrael discovered two guests seated at a lavishly decorated table set with a white tablecloth, china plates, bowls of flowers, and tall candles that flickered in the soft night breeze.

Azrael's brows lifted as he caught sight of the stunted gargoyle who was quickly wearing on his nerves, and the male's pretty Aunt Bertha, who was currently wearing a sparkly silver gown with her golden hair in an elaborate knot on top of her head. The two couldn't have been more different, but there was something strangely similar about them. Maybe it was the tilt of their heads or the flash of their smiles.

Or perhaps it was their mutual ability to walk into a room and cause complete chaos.

Still, it wasn't the odd couple that caught and held Azrael's attention. It was the redheaded vampire dressed in a waiter's uniform, standing next to the table as he poured wine for Bertha and then Levet.

The gargoyle took the glass, giving it a suspicious sniff before shoving the glass back to the scowling Gideon.

"This is pig swill. Bring us your finest champagne."

Gideon's fangs were fully extended, the air vibrating with his icy fury as he spun on his heel and headed for the door to the wine cellars.

"Oh, you're evil," he whispered, wrapping his arms around Jayla's waist.

She tilted back her head, her dark hair rippling over her shoulders. "Evil in a good way? Or evil in a bad way?"

"In the very best way," he said in approving tones. "Gideon looks like he's considering the benefits of setting himself on fire."

"I have plenty of torches to help." She nodded toward the glowing flames that surrounded the patio. "I'll set him aflame myself if it speeds things along."

Azrael chuckled. His fierce assassin. "Why the lavish dinner?"

"Bertha is leaving later tonight." Jayla shrugged. "She says that she's been summoned by a mystical force."

"I don't suppose she's taking that lump of granite with her?" Azrael asked. So far, Levet had managed to piss off the chef when he stole a platter of roasted ducks, he'd scorched the carpets in Jayla's private rooms while trying to impress her by juggling his fireballs, and interrupted their privacy with tedious regularity.

"I don't think so."

"Damn." He tightened his arms around her waist, his fangs lengthening as he gazed down at her pale, perfect face. "I want you all to myself."

A slow smile of invitation curved her lips. "Everything seems to be under control here if you're in the mood to rip off my dress."

With a growl, he swept her off her feet and headed into the darkness with blinding speed. "The second I'm not in the mood, you can set me on fire with one of those torches," he assured her.

Her arms wrapped around his neck. "Deal."

* * * *

Also from 1001 Dark Nights and Alexandra Ivy, discover Sacrifice of Darkness, Blade, Rage/Killian and Kayden/Simon.

Sign up for the 1001 Dark Nights Newsletter
and be entered to win a Tiffany Key necklace.

There's a contest every month!

Go to www.1001DarkNights.com to subscribe.

**As a bonus, all subscribers can download
FIVE FREE exclusive books!**

Discover 1001 Dark Nights Collection Eight

DRAGON REVEALED by Donna Grant
A Dragon Kings Novella

CAPTURED IN INK by Carrie Ann Ryan
A Montgomery Ink: Boulder Novella

SECURING JANE by Susan Stoker
A SEAL of Protection: Legacy Series Novella

WILD WIND by Kristen Ashley
A Chaos Novella

DARE TO TEASE by Carly Phillips
A Dare Nation Novella

VAMPIRE by Rebecca Zanetti
A Dark Protectors/Rebels Novella

MAFIA KING by Rachel Van Dyken
A Mafia Royals Novella

THE GRAVEDIGGER'S SON by Darynda Jones
A Charley Davidson Novella

FINALE by Skye Warren
A North Security Novella

MEMORIES OF YOU by J. Kenner
A Stark Securities Novella

SLAYED BY DARKNESS by Alexandra Ivy
A Guardians of Eternity Novella

TREASURED by Lexi Blake
A Masters and Mercenaries Novella

THE DAREDEVIL by Dylan Allen
A Rivers Wilde Novella

BOND OF DESTINY by Larissa Ione
A Demonica Novella

THE CLOSE-UP by Kennedy Ryan
A Hollywood Renaissance Novella

MORE THAN POSSESS YOU by Shayla Black
A More Than Words Novella

HAUNTED HOUSE by Heather Graham
A Krewe of Hunters Novella

MAN FOR ME by Laurelin Paige
A Man In Charge Novella

THE RHYTHM METHOD by Kylie Scott
A Stage Dive Novella

JONAH BENNETT by Tijan
A Bennett Mafia Novella

CHANGE WITH ME by Kristen Proby
A With Me In Seattle Novella

THE DARKEST DESTINY by Gena Showalter
A Lords of the Underworld Novella

Also from Blue Box Press

THE LAST TIARA by M.J. Rose

THE CROWN OF GILDED BONES by Jennifer L. Armentrout
A Blood and Ash Novel

THE MISSING SISTER by Lucinda Riley

Discover More Alexandra Ivy

Sacrifice of Darkness
A Guardians of Eternity Novella
By Alexandra Ivy

Javad has one rule. No fighting pits.

It doesn't matter that the savage battles have been a tradition among demons for eons. As the manager of the Viper's Nest in Vegas, his word is law. Period. Then he hears rumors that some fool has dared to create a fighting pit in the middle of the desert. He goes in search of the hidden location, only to realize too late it's a trap by his former master Vynom. The powerful vampire is determined to force Javad to fight once again. This time to the death.

Terra is a rare fey creature known as a Seraf. Long ago she'd been captured by Vynom and forced to heal the fighters he used in his pits. Javad had rescued her, and she'd given him a medallion. If he ever needed her, all he had to do was to speak her name and the magic would lead her to him. When she hears his call she doesn't hesitate to rush to his rescue. Even when it means returning to the dark violence that still haunts her dreams.

Can they escape the nightmare that nearly destroyed them in the past? And if they survive, are they willing to sacrifice the duties that have pulled them apart to battle for a future together?

* * * *

Blade
A Bayou Heat Novella
By Alexandra Ivy & Laura Wright

Sexy Suit, Blade was held captive and abused for decades. Benson Enterprises was desperate to use his superior blood to create super soldiers. But when he's finally rescued, he can't return to the Wildlands with the other prisoners. Not without the female he was forced to watch being impregnated. The female who has gone missing.

Beautiful and broken, Valli just wants to run away and never look back. But with the shocking news of her pregnancy fresh in her mind, she wonders if that's even possible. Told by her captors that one of the caged animals assaulted her, she knows she must do everything in her power to keep her unborn child safe. But when a glorious male tracks her down and claims her and her baby as his own, will she have the strength to walk away?

* * * *

Rage/Killian
Bayou Heat Novellas
By Alexandra Ivy and Laura Wright

RAGE

Rage might be an aggressive Hunter by nature, but the gorgeous male has never had a problem charming the females. All except Lucie Gaudet. Of course, the lovely Geek is a born troublemaker, and it was no surprise to Rage when she was kicked out of the Wildlands.

But now the Pantera need a first-class hacker to stop the potential destruction of their people. And it's up to Rage to convince Lucie to help. Can the two forget the past—and their sizzling attraction—to save the Pantera?

KILLIAN

Gorgeous, brutal, aggressive, and *human*, Killian O'Roarke wants only two things: to get rid of the Pantera DNA he's been infected with, and get back to the field. But the decorated Army Ranger never bargained on meeting the woman—the female—of his dreams on his mission to the Wildlands.

Rosalie lost her mate to a human, and now the Hunter despises them all. In fact, she thinks they're good for only one thing: barbeque. But this one she's guarding is testing her beliefs. He is proud and kind, and also knows the pain of loss. But in a time of war between their species, isn't any chance of love destined for destruction?

* * * *

Kayden/Simon
Bayou Heat Novellas
By Alexandra Ivy & Laura Wright

ENEMY TO LOVER:

Kayden is obsessed with revenge after his parents disappeared when he was just a cub. Now the gorgeous Hunter has discovered the man responsible for betraying them - Joshua Ford - and it's time for payback. Beginning with the kidnapping of Joshua's daughter, Bianca. But last thing he expects is to be confronted with the horrifying realization that Bianca is his mate. Will he put revenge before his chance for eternal happiness?

BEAUTY AND THE BEAST

Sexy male model, Simon refuses to give up his exciting life in New York City to return to the slow heat of the Wildlands. For a decade, many Pantera have tried to capture the rogue Diplomat and bring him home, but all have failed. Now it's Tryst's turn. The hard, brilliant, and gorgeous, Hunter is the ultimate tracker. But can the admitted beast-girl of the Wildlands capture her prey without losing her heart in the process?

Bewitch the Darkness

Guardians of Eternity Book 18
By Alexandra Ivy
Coming November 16, 2021

The vampires and werewolves chosen to be the Guardians of Eternity believe they've conquered their latest threat. But as one of them will learn in this mesmerizing installment from *New York Times* bestselling author Alexandra Ivy, old lovers make the most ruthless new enemies…

Only one drastic mission can tempt Kyi away from the peaceful woodland where the dryads raised her: killing her mother. Xuria's beauty masks a bone-deep evil that has enslaved fey for centuries with the help of a powerful stone. A hundred years ago, Kyi almost succeeded—until one meddlesome vampire destroyed her chance. With rumors that Xuria has emerged from her secret realm, Kyi's determined to try again—despite the vampire who is now focused on destroying her.

Locke has been waiting over a century to avenge what he believes was Xuria's death. Discovering the sorceress's raven-haired fey daughter was the assassin is a surprise—until her story of Xuria's treachery begins to ring true. Working with Kyi is one solution—and the relentless heat simmering between them is a hint that they may be fated as mates. But even a destined love will have to wait as they now struggle to defeat Kyi's twin sister, who has a chilling plan of her own…

* * * *

"Are you looking for me?" Styx demanded when the male continued to stand there, eying him with an inscrutable expression.

"Yes."

"Then what are you waiting on? An engraved invitation?"

Xi's dark gaze drifted around the room before returning to Styx. "I'm attempting to decide whether or not I have the courage to enter."

Styx scowled. He'd witnessed this male battle a horde of orcs with nothing more than his fangs and a dagger.

"The one thing you've never lacked is courage, amigo."

"Normally I would agree with you, but you have been…"

Styx lifted his six-foot five body out of the chair. "I've been what?"

"Volatile over the past weeks," Xi told him.

The Raven was right. The past month had stretched Styx's limited patience to the breaking point. It was nothing he could put his finger on. Unexplained fires. Sudden riots. Vandalism. Brutal attacks on lesser demons.

Every night he woke to discover a line of demons waiting to make a complaint or plead for his assistance. It was enough to stress out the most Zen vampire. And there was nothing Zen about Styx.

Which was why he'd requested Xi to investigate the various incidents.

With an effort, Styx leashed his burst of annoyance at the interruption. He even managed to force a wry smile to his lips.

"According to my mate I'm always volatile."

Xi didn't argue. "More volatile than usual," he clarified.

"Mount Etna volatile or Mount Vesuvius?"

Xi answered without hesitation. "Definitely Mount Vesuvius."

Styx tapped a finger on the edge of his desk. He was often short-tempered. It was part of his charm. But the past month had rubbed his nerves raw.

"I've had a stressful times, terrifying times, and the world-is-about-to-end times. But this…" He shook his head. "I feel like I'm being tormented by a thousand unseen ants. Each biting when I least expect it."

"The city is seething."

"Seething. Yes. That's exactly what's happening," Styx agreed. It was like they were sitting on a simmering pot that might boil over at any moment. "I don't suppose you've managed to discover what's causing the trouble?"

"I have answers for the latest incidents." Xi strolled forward, halting next to the desk. "The collapse at the sanctuary happened when the wooden beams in the ceiling shattered."

The sanctuary had been Darcy's idea. She'd spent years barely scraping by, unaware why she was different from other people. She wanted a place for demons to go that would offer them food and a warm place to sleep, as well as protection from the more predator demons. Or even from humans who had a tendency to kill what they feared.

A week ago, the old warehouse collapsed into a pile of rubble, wounding several of those seeking asylum. Darcy had been furious and

Styx had promised to get to the bottom of the collapse.

"Did someone tamper with them?" he asked Xi.

The Raven shrugged. "The damage was too great to determine if it was an accident or deliberate."

Styx was willing to bet it was deliberate. "And the others?"

"The fire at the Viper Club was caused by an electrical surge," Xi continued. "And the rampaging vampire that we captured claims he was kidnapped and injected with some unknown toxin that sent him into a psychotic episode."

It'd only been a night ago that Styx had received a frantic call that warned there was a crazed vampire destroying a human nightclub. The male was not only creating chaos, but he was threatening to expose the existence of vampires. Something that would be catastrophic for the entire demon world.

Styx had personally gone to the club to capture the idiot and toss him in a locked cell. It was also when he'd suggested to Darcy she might want to visit her sister. Anything to get her out of town.

"Where was he kidnapped from?" Styx demanded.

"In front of your lair."

Styx hissed in outrage. What demon had the balls to kidnap a vampire beneath the nose of the Anasso?

A dead one.

About Alexandra Ivy

Alexandra Ivy graduated from Truman University with a degree in theatre before deciding she preferred to bring her characters to life on paper rather than stage. She started her career writing traditional regencies before moving into the world of paranormal with her USA Today, Wall Street Journal, and New York Times bestselling series The Guardians of Eternity. Now she writes a wide variety of genres that include paranormal, erotica, and romantic suspense.

Text ALEXANDRA to 24587 to receive text alerts whenever a new release comes out!

Visit https://alexandraivy.com for more information.

Discover 1001 Dark Nights

TRICKED by Rebecca Zanetti ~ DIRTY WICKED by Shayla Black ~ THE ONLY ONE by Lauren Blakely ~ SWEET SURRENDER by Liliana Hart

COLLECTION FOUR
ROCK CHICK REAWAKENING by Kristen Ashley ~ ADORING INK by Carrie Ann Ryan ~ SWEET RIVALRY by K. Bromberg ~ SHADE'S LADY by Joanna Wylde ~ RAZR by Larissa Ione ~ ARRANGED by Lexi Blake ~ TANGLED by Rebecca Zanetti ~ HOLD ME by J. Kenner ~ SOMEHOW, SOME WAY by Jennifer Probst ~ TOO CLOSE TO CALL by Tessa Bailey ~ HUNTED by Elisabeth Naughton ~ EYES ON YOU by Laura Kaye ~ BLADE by Alexandra Ivy/Laura Wright ~ DRAGON BURN by Donna Grant ~ TRIPPED OUT by Lorelei James ~ STUD FINDER by Lauren Blakely ~ MIDNIGHT UNLEASHED by Lara Adrian ~ HALLOW BE THE HAUNT by Heather Graham ~ DIRTY FILTHY FIX by Laurelin Paige ~ THE BED MATE by Kendall Ryan ~ NIGHT GAMES by CD Reiss ~ NO RESERVATIONS by Kristen Proby ~ DAWN OF SURRENDER by Liliana Hart

COLLECTION FIVE
BLAZE ERUPTING by Rebecca Zanetti ~ ROUGH RIDE by Kristen Ashley ~ HAWKYN by Larissa Ione ~ RIDE DIRTY by Laura Kaye ~ ROME'S CHANCE by Joanna Wylde ~ THE MARRIAGE ARRANGEMENT by Jennifer Probst ~ SURRENDER by Elisabeth Naughton ~ INKED NIGHTS by Carrie Ann Ryan ~ ENVY by Rachel Van Dyken ~ PROTECTED by Lexi Blake ~ THE PRINCE by Jennifer L. Armentrout ~ PLEASE ME by J. Kenner ~ WOUND TIGHT by Lorelei James ~ STRONG by Kylie Scott ~ DRAGON NIGHT by Donna Grant ~ TEMPTING BROOKE by Kristen Proby ~ HAUNTED BE THE HOLIDAYS by Heather Graham ~ CONTROL by K. Bromberg ~ HUNKY HEARTBREAKER by Kendall Ryan ~ THE DARKEST CAPTIVE by Gena Showalter

COLLECTION SIX
DRAGON CLAIMED by Donna Grant ~ ASHES TO INK by Carrie Ann Ryan ~ ENSNARED by Elisabeth Naughton ~ EVERMORE by Corinne Michaels ~ VENGEANCE by Rebecca Zanetti ~ ELI'S TRIUMPH by Joanna Wylde ~ CIPHER by Larissa Ione ~

RESCUING MACIE by Susan Stoker ~ ENCHANTED by Lexi Blake ~ TAKE THE BRIDE by Carly Phillips ~ INDULGE ME by J. Kenner ~ THE KING by Jennifer L. Armentrout ~ QUIET MAN by Kristen Ashley ~ ABANDON by Rachel Van Dyken ~ THE OPEN DOOR by Laurelin Paige ~ CLOSER by Kylie Scott ~ SOMETHING JUST LIKE THIS by Jennifer Probst ~ BLOOD NIGHT by Heather Graham ~ TWIST OF FATE by Jill Shalvis ~ MORE THAN PLEASURE YOU by Shayla Black ~ WONDER WITH ME by Kristen Proby ~ THE DARKEST ASSASSIN by Gena Showalter

COLLECTION SEVEN
THE BISHOP by Skye Warren ~ TAKEN WITH YOU by Carrie Ann Ryan ~ DRAGON LOST by Donna Grant ~ SEXY LOVE by Carly Phillips ~ PROVOKE by Rachel Van Dyken ~ RAFE by Sawyer Bennett ~ THE NAUGHTY PRINCESS by Claire Contreras ~ THE GRAVEYARD SHIFT by Darynda Jones ~ CHARMED by Lexi Blake ~ SACRIFICE OF DARKNESS by Alexandra Ivy ~ THE QUEEN by Jen Armentrout ~ BEGIN AGAIN by Jennifer Probst ~ VIXEN by Rebecca Zanetti ~ SLASH by Laurelin Paige ~ THE DEAD HEAT OF SUMMER by Heather Graham ~ WILD FIRE by Kristen Ashley ~ MORE THAN PROTECT YOU by Shayla Black ~ LOVE SONG by Kylie Scott ~ CHERISH ME by J. Kenner ~ SHINE WITH ME by Kristen Proby

Discover Blue Box Press
TAME ME by J. Kenner ~ TEMPT ME by J. Kenner ~ DAMIEN by J. Kenner ~ TEASE ME by J. Kenner ~ REAPER by Larissa Ione ~ THE SURRENDER GATE by Christopher Rice ~ SERVICING THE TARGET by Cherise Sinclair ~ THE LAKE OF LEARNING by Steve Berry and MJ Rose ~ THE MUSEUM OF MYSTERIES by Steve Berry and MJ Rose ~ TEASE ME by J. Kenner ~ FROM BLOOD AND ASH by Jennifer L. Armentrout ~ QUEEN MOVE by Kennedy Ryan ~ THE HOUSE OF LONG AGO by Steve Berry and MJ Rose ~ THE BUTTERFLY ROOM by Lucinda Riley ~ A KINGDOM OF FLESH AND FIRE by Jennifer L. Armentrout

On Behalf of 1001 Dark Nights,

Liz Berry, M.J. Rose, and Jillian Stein would like to thank ~

Steve Berry
Doug Scofield
Benjamin Stein
Kim Guidroz
Social Butterfly PR
Ashley Wells
Asha Hossain
Chris Graham
Chelle Olson
Kasi Alexander
Jessica Johns
Dylan Stockton
Richard Blake
and Simon Lipskar

Made in the USA
Las Vegas, NV
20 June 2021